THE DAY OF THE HELLION

Jim Ames arrived home to discover that Laurel Bergen, his intended bride, had become involved with his old enemy, Rex Mills, he could have forgiven that, but after his father was murdered Laurel went riding off into a stormy evening. Ames followed her on to the Medicine Bow. There he sat in the darkness of the forest night and heard Laurel and some badmen talking. What they said made little sense, but light did finally dawn when Ames learned of the kidnapped Mary Frayleson.

THE DAY OF THE HELLION

THE DAY OF THE HELLION

by
Jeff Blaine

Dales Large Print Books
Long Preston, North Yorkshire,
England.

British Library Cataloguing in Publication Data.

Blaine, Jeff
    The day of the hellion.

A catalogue record for this book is
available from the British Library

ISBN 1-85389-495-8 pbk

First published in Great Britain by Robert Hale Ltd., 1992

Published in Large Print 1994 by arrangement with Robert
Hale Ltd.

Dales Large Print is an imprint of
Library Magna Books Ltd.
Printed and bound in Great Britain by
T.J. Press (Padstow) Ltd., Cornwall, PL28 8RW.

ONE

Jim Ames was angry, and getting more so by the moment. He was in fact so angry that his tongue was beginning to run away with him, and the fury of his words reached what could only be described as the totally unacceptable when he bawled: 'I'm gong to kill him, pa! He's done with his petticoat-chasing ways! I'm going out there right now, and I'm gong to find and kill the skunk!'

'You hold it right there, Jimmy!' warned Hank Ames, his father, the older man's stern voice fairly cracking through the charged atmosphere of the room. 'You seem to have forgotten that I'm the sheriff of this town. I won't listen to that kind of talk from the folk outside, so I'm damned sure I'm not going to listen to it in my own home. And especially not from my son, who's plenty old enough to know better!' He sat bolt upright in his chair, greying features painfully creased and almost pleading as he looked up at his son and heir. 'What's up with you, boy? This is the first time you've been home in over a year, and you're no sooner into the parlour than you start raging like a wild man. Now it's talk of murder! It ain't like you, Jimmy, and that's a fact. What's happened to change you so much?'

'I'm the same man I always was,' Jim Ames retorted, his voice much lower and more controlled now but filled with a bitter sadness nevertheless. 'Pa, I began this day the happiest of men. I was in the best of moods. I was on my way home, and the thought of seeing you and the things in my room again made me want to sing out loud. I figured the worst was over for me. I'd got my start in life and, after a happy time here, I reckoned to ride back to Cheyenne with Laury at my side, pick up my job as I'd left it, get a home started, and then make a real good life for that girl and me.'

'All right,' Hank Ames said, as his son paused and swallowed hard. 'Everything's in order so far. Then what happened?'

'I'll tell you what happened,' the younger man went on grimly. 'I rode into Brayton, and that fat fool, Morg Darley, sprang out from behind a bush, grabbed my mount at the bit, and informed me that Laurel Bergen, my girl, had become the talk of the place through her downright wanton behaviour with that long galoot, Rex Mills. Darley was plain gloating when he told me that that pair had actually been seen doing what they shouldn't up in the pinewoods. Oh, sure, pa! We all know about Morg! He's daft as he is wicked! But I knew he'd told me the truth the moment I got into the middle of this town of ours and I saw a bunch of friends of mine from the old days laughing at me dirtily behind their hands. Do you wonder I'm upset, pa? I staked my all on Laury, and it sure as hell looks like she's betrayed me!'

'Betrayed you?' Hank Ames wondered, shaking his head at his son. 'You'd better get these things straight in your skull, Jimmy. You and Laurel Bergen were not officially engaged. You and her had an understanding—that's all. Your girl? She'd proved before Rex Mills she wasn't quite that! And well you knew it.' He looked his son straight in the eye, letting the words sink in. 'Fact is, boy, there are no gentlemen's agreements between male and female. Each partakes of his or her own nature, as they say; and, short of

9

being hog-tied, will go on following out what they are. Laury was never any better than she ought to be, but that's her affair. When you left for Cheyenne, there was no commitment, and you've just got to accept anything that's happened since. Be a man about it, son! Only lovesick kids fly off the handle when they find the other party ain't as faithful as they'd like.'

'Easy for you to talk, pa!'

'Jimmy, most of us have to suffer some such in our time,' Hank Ames sighed, shaking his head at his son's reproach. 'Life's always been the same, though it seems bright and fresh to each new generation. Can you accept a fact that's self-evident? We ain't all gifted alike with looks and charms. Handsome men and beautiful women are granted a kind of licence that's denied most of us. Don't matter much what they do that's heart-breaking, there's always a new partner waiting round the corner. If you've set your cap at a beautiful woman, my bucko, competition is what you've got to expect! If you want the girl, you'll have to play out the game. Did you really expect a filly of Laurel Bergen's cut to sit at home and sew while you were away? Some hopes

10

you'd got! Rex Mills was just waiting for the chance to muscle in. And that's what he did.'

Jim Ames began to protest anew.

But his father cut him short with a wave of the hand. 'Don't tell me—don't tell! Your going away was as much for the girl's benefit as your own. That job as a bank guard in Cheyenne sure offered fine prospects to the right man, and I'd say you've proved yourself that. Sadly, however, looked at from the woman's point of view—and there never was a female who looked at it from any other—you went away and left her. Son, you're no hand at writing either. Even your late mother used to—'

'I wrote letters!' Jim Ames interrupted hotly.

'Oh, yeah! How many?'

'Well—'

'Two,' his father completed for him. 'Laury told me about them. Such long letters. Each one had about six lines to it.'

'It's true I'm no hand with a pen,' Jim Ames admitted. 'No man's good at everything.'

'The fact is, son,' the older man said

deliberately, 'you're most to blame for what's happened to you here. It's that female viewpoint, d'you see? You can never ignore it. Laury felt herself deserted, and that's a pay-back situation for a pretty girl. So it's my guess Miss Bergen has been paying you back in your absence how she knew it would eventually hurt you most. And she sure has hurt you!'

'I wouldn't have thought it of her,' Jim Ames growled, chilled by the suddenly perceived truth of it and seeing clearly now. 'But I find it hard to believe it was all that.'

'Perhaps not,' Hank Ames conceded, frowning thoughtfully to himself. 'Laury needs a man, son. She's built that way. Sure, other men will laugh at you on that account—and it does give pain. Though mostly to a man's pride. So don't let it show. You'll only be a real loser, Jimmy, if you leave them saying you couldn't take it.'

'Leave here?'

'If you like.'

'There's not much else to do but leave,' Jim Ames reflected wryly. 'With Laury out of my plans, there's nothing in Baytown for me. It's the butt end of nowhere, and not a patch on Cheyenne for anything. Besides, ma's lying in the cemetery and you're on duty when you're not asleep.'

Hank Ames nodded slowly, his attention turned inwards again. 'Son, I want a straight answer to a straight question. It's asked in all sincerity mind.'

'Shoot.'

'Does Laurel Bergen being light of the leg trouble you as deep as it goes? Remembering many a girl who's been no better than she should has gone on to make a good and faithful wife?'

'I guess not, pa,' Jim Ames confided. 'Who's been that perfect?'

Hank Ames passed a look over his son's face and gave a knowing grin. 'If you came by the chance then, you'd take Laury out of Brayton as soon as you could?'

'That's what I came for.'

'Stick around as long as you can, Jimmy,' his father advised. 'I've got troubles of my own. Troubles at work. But they could iron out in such manner as to help you some. Might even put things right for you entirely. We'll have to wait and see about that. I'll know more when my new deputy, Frank Broom, gets down from the Medicine Bow. It's home country to him up there, and he's doing some special investigating for me.'

'What's this?' Jim Ames asked curiously.

'The day of the hellion maybe,' his father replied gravely, looking at the clock on the mantelpiece and then heaving himself out of his chair. 'I can't say a lot more now. Suffice to add that I believe Rex Mills has become something more than a wild young fool, and that a good fright might just jolt Miss Bergen into thinking straight.' Now he picked up his Stetson off a nearby straight-backed chair and set it on his head, pulling it to the exact angle that suited him best. 'You know where the pantry is, Jimmy, and everything else in the house. I've touched little since your mother left us. Make yourself at home.'

'Okay,' Jim Ames said, moving aside to give his father a clear path to the door that connected the parlour with the hall. 'Thanks, pa.'

Hank Ames paused in the doorway, a six-foot man, with square, muscular shoulders, solid hips, and lean round limbs that were still full of strength at fifty-odd, the obvious original model of which his son now stood the perfect specimen. 'Feeling better?'

'Reckon it's all off my chest, pa.'

The older man nodded sagaciously. 'See it doesn't boil up again. These grievances do sometimes.'

Jim Ames nodded wryly. 'Sure did go off there, didn't I? It was all hot air.'

Hank Ames gave him a long, hard look, then a faint smile. 'Don't forget what I told you. I *am* the sheriff of Brayton.' He fished out his pocket watch on this occasion, thumbing open its silver face-cover. 'Yes, and it's now long past time that I got back to my office and started behaving like it. Typical case of a lunch break turning into a dinner hour. So long, Jimmy.'

Jim Ames raised a hand, and his father vanished into the shadows of the hall and then left the house, closing the front door quietly behind him.

Walking to the armchair opposite the one that his parent had so recently vacated, Ames sank down into it and made himself as comfortable as he could. Tipping back his head, he gazed at the ceiling and was conscious of the trembling that still persisted in the fibres of his being. That had been a pretty shameful performance which he had lately put on, and his father had proved a remarkably understanding man. Tolerant indeed. For every word

15

that Henry Ames had spoken concerning his son's lack of self-control had been true. He, Jim, should never have allowed himself to be provoked by that idiot, Morgan Darley. He had given in to a sense of disappointment and sheer sexual jealousy where he should have felt neither. A man who had been brought up right didn't dwell upon these matters, but he had always known that Laury Bergen was often active in a way that she shouldn't be active. There had been fellows ahead of Rex Mills, and Ames had always felt that he respected the girl to no purpose—and, perhaps, her secret amusement. That was what love did for you. Yet deep down, it had been his awareness of Laury's natural inconstancy that had restrained him from pressing the girl for any true commitment before he had left Brayton for Cheyenne. He had hoped she would stay faithful, but it appeared she hadn't, and that was that. He was hurt, yet not really surprised. Nor had her latest behaviour altered his feelings for her in any respect. Laury was simply Laury. Everything about her was right for him. Her auburn hair, those bold features, that hour-glass figure, the sweet laughter in her voice, and the firm touch of her fingertips on his flesh. The sum total of these things—with a flavour or two more subtle—made her the fulfilment of his personal dream of womanhood. He'd go on wanting her even if he knew that she had first been handed down through all the devils in hell. There was the strength and the weakness of his nature; and he would do wisely to accept it and forget the rest.

Still conscious that his inner self was overtaut, Ames stood up again and stretched himself hard, walking twice round the room after that and stopping again at much the same spot from which he had started. Now he considered the other matters of which his father had spoken, but they had really been too vague to make any real impact on his mind and he was reminded that his pa had always had a tendency to ramble and imply where there had been nothing to ramble and imply about. The day of the hellion, eh? When had there ever been a day that wasn't the day of the hellion? Human tolerance had always given evil a head start, and men didn't improve much with the ages. Fellows like the handsome and uncaring Rex Mills would always be dubious quantities. Better forget that too.

Yet it would be a good thing on the purely practical level if he could take Laury away from Mills. Perhaps she would come for the asking. It would be worth the question. Anyhow, he realized that he could in some measure be presupposing failure with the girl, since he had no idea of his exact status with her at this time. In fact he could be leaning too hard on his father's analysis of what had occurred in Laury's mind concerning him. Sure, pa had had the more recent advantage of talking with her, but that didn't cover everything. Laury was changeable. Be damned if he wouldn't go and see her right now! He didn't think they would grudge him a minute or two of her time along at the Hillwood Stage and Freight Office where she worked. Once he had spoken with the girl, he would at least have a clearer idea of how she felt towards him—and most of his future doings would automatically emerge from that.

Ames left the house without more ado and, looking up, pushed the key into the space under the doorstep where it had always been hidden. Then, stepping out of the garden gate, he turned right and walked up the street, as ever feeling overshadowed

18

by the mountains that reared along the western skyline and likewise soothed by the essential greenness of the nearer foothills and pine forests. He cast an eye across the black ribs and snow-whitened ramparts of the Medicine Bow—a formless thought about his father's deputy, Frank Broom, flickering briefly in his mind—and then the familiar shapes of the buildings on either side of the way claimed his whole attention, and he gazed towards the newly painted front of the Hillwood establishment, with its wide gateway to the freight yard at the back of the place situated on the left of the erection and the big glass window that served the office itself looking out from the side wall facing him and directly upon the entrance.

Crossing the street, Ames moved closer to the broad gateway, spotting movement behind the nearby window, and he glimpsed an auburn-haired figure—who could only be Laurel Bergen—busying herself at a desk, her back turned squarely towards him. Halting, he received an uneasy impression that the girl had seen him before he had seen her and promptly turned away in an effort to convey the idea that she didn't know he was out there on the street. It was disconcerting—and the more so because he realized that he was in a hypersensitive state and could be mistaken—but his feeling about the girl's prior knowledge of his presence intensified when she failed to glance outside on turning away from the desk and walked out of the office and deeper into the building with a pile of papers and holdalls in her hands.

Ames set his arms akimbo. He began waiting hesitantly against the girl's return. But the office remained empty of her presence and he soon started forming the notion that Laury would not reappear at her desk until he had taken himself off. This conviction quickly grew and was markedly intensified when, on the impulse, he looked upwards and saw a drape at a window high above him quiver slightly as a hand was withdrawn from it. Yes, Laury knew he was down here all right, and he reckoned she intended to keep out of the way for as long as it took. He sighed, grinding his teeth in vexation. Damn the girl! She was being silly! They would have to meet sooner or later. She must know that. Well, perhaps it was that she didn't wish to be interrupted at her work, and he supposed that he owed her the courtesy of accepting that as the explanation of it for now. But it made him feel even more uncomfortable, and his apprehension for the future became acute.

He turned away, for a body had to keep some pride. No drinking man as a rule, he suddenly felt the need for a drink—a strong one; whisky. And he walked across the road, kicking stones, and shouldered through the batwings of Johnsons's Bar, his progress taking him up to the divide itself, where he halted the clenched fists upon the battered oak and rasped out his request for a bottle of Old Crow as a lean, gingery, English-looking bartender approached him somewhat diffidently. The bottle was duly supplied, the barman pouring the first drink, and Ames shoved a couple of dollars across the divide and then carried glass and bottle to a table from which he had a good view of the street but none of the window in the Hillwood building behind which Laurel Bergen had probably returned to her work again by now.

Seating himself, Ames tossed his drink back, then poured another, and had begun rolling his glass in his fingers and idly studying its contents, when a tall, lantern-jawed man leaned over him and said: 'As I live and breathe—Jim Ames!'

Ames glanced up into the other's high-cheekboned face, his manner faintly challenging. 'Hello, Vestry. Why the surprise? I haven't been away for years.'

'Maybe not then,' the other admitted. 'I suppose a man is allowed to be glad to see you?'

'When were you ever glad to see me?' Ames asked, showing amused incredulity, for Claude Vestry was Rex Mills' bosom pal and an individual with whom he'd had a number of fistfights back in their schooldays—always winning, but only just. 'What d'you want?'

'Must I want something?' Vestry inquired, holding out his whisky glass. 'If you're being sociable?'

Ames filled Vestry's glass, then raised his own in salute and swallowed half its contents.

'Ames,' the other acknowledged.

'Sit down if you want to.'

Vestry hooked up a chair and sat down. 'Back for Laury?'

'That was the idea.'

'Was?'

'You know what I mean, mister,' Ames said, unwilling to risk starting trouble as yet by telling Vestry to mind his own business. 'Less of the innocence, please.'

'You mustn't mind old Rex.'

'No?'

'Story of the wasp and the pot of jam.'

'The wasp finally got stuck.'

Vestry pulled a wry jib, scratching deep into a shaggy sideburn. 'Good job?'

'The one in Cheyenne? Yes. Real good.'

'Heard you were gunning it at the Stockman's Bank.'

'You heard right.'

'Guarding gold shipments sometimes.'

'You heard right again.'

'Should suit Laury down to the ground,' Vestry observed. 'Maybe your manager can find a place for her. She's a great one at totting up. Her boss reckons she ain't made a mistake at the freight office all the years she's worked for him.'

'I can believe that,' Ames said, filling Vestry's glass again, as much because he'd just bought all this booze and no longer wanted it as anything else. 'I'll have another job for her—if I get her to Cheyenne.'

'Never say die, man.'

'What do you know about it?'

'Never say die,' Vestry repeated, drinking with relish. 'Sure hits the spot.'

'What are you doing these days, Claude?' Ames inquired, having consumed just enough of the ninety-six proof spirit to find his own tongue loosened. 'Up to any good?'

'Was that meant to be a joke?' Vestry asked a trifle stiffly. 'I'm a miner.'

'Rex too?'

'Him too.'

'Different from what I heard.'

'What have you heard?' Vestry gritted tightly. 'Your father's been opening his mouth.'

'Afraid of the truth, Claude?' Ames wondered, suddenly conscious of movement on the street beyond the bar-room window and his companion pointing.

'Speak of the devil,' Vestry cried a little drunkenly, 'and his imps will appear!'

Ames saw that it was his father walking by and guessed that his parent was doing one of the law's many obligatory rounds of Brayton for the day; and he was reflecting on the underlying boredom of the older man's lot, when a rifle shot boomed and Hank Ames came to an abrupt halt and buckled to the ground.

Jim Ames was off his chair in an instant, and would have been out through the batwings in another, but suddenly his legs encountered a tripping foot and over he went onto his face.

TWO

Between the mental shock of what he had just witnessed—and the physical one of coming to rest on the point of his chin after what amounted to an unchecked fall—Ames lay upon his belly in a three-parts senseless state for several moments before a pair of strong hands jerked him off the floor boards and set him upon his feet. 'I'm real sorry, Ames,' he heard Claude Vestry say in his ear, 'but you fell over my leg.'

Ames sucked in a breath that filled his chest to the limit. Shaking off the supporting hands, he felt instinctively that the trip had been no accident, but this was not the time for recriminations and he dived for the street, bursting through the swing-doors and then crossing the ground to his father's side. Here, praying for signs of life, he turned the fallen man off his face and peered closely, but Hank Ames stared blankly back at him. Dark blood welled slowly from a big hole near the centre of the sheriff's chest, and it was obvious that his heart had been shot through. The lawman was as dead as a man could be.

Numb from cowlick to toenails, Ames tried to think coherently, but no fragment of his thinking held firm. Instinctively, he turned full circle, his eyes searching rooftops and alley ends that were but half seen in his present state. He really had little idea of what he sought, and came to a stop once more with his gaze again turned down upon his father's body. Nor did he react when a heavy, black-suited figure elbowed him aside and then sank into a kneeling position at Hank Ames's right hip, a stethoscope hanging before him and a medical bag in his left hand. It occurred to Ames that Doc Rutherford must have been close by when the shot had been fired and might have done much good in propitious circumstances—but Ames knew that the man could do nothing here and simply stood by, his shock ebbing now, and waited for the medico to admit the fact of it.

Rutherford did a thorough job with his stethoscope, then stood up and put a consoling hand on Ames's right shoulder. 'I'm sorry, Jimmy. He couldn't have known what hit him.'

'It's all right, doc,' Ames heard himself say stonily. 'I've seen dead men before.'

'That's right, Jimmy,' the rubicund doctor said, 'try to keep a cool head about it.'

'But, doc, it was murder,' Ames insisted. 'He was deliberately shot down.'

'It certainly appears that way,' Rutherford admitted reluctantly.

'Appears?' Ames echoed, anger blurting through him. 'You were on the street —must have been. Didn't you see who did it?'

'I saw nothing,' the doctor replied. 'That is to say, I saw your father fall, up street of me, as I turned my horse and buggy out of my gateway back there.'

'But you had a full view of the street!'

'Yes.'

'And you saw nothing?'

'Nothing,' Rutherford agreed, momentarily curt. 'I'll have to tell Deputy Sheriff

27

Broom exactly the same—when he comes to investigate what happened here.'

'I don't know this man Broom,' Ames said. 'Never met him. He must be new about here. Anyway, my father told me not an hour ago that Broom isn't in town. How come you didn't see anything?'

'I didn't, that's all,' Rutherford said, his tones now emphasizing that his patience was under strain. 'Yes, I had the whole main street open before me, but I saw nobody upon it.'

'Somebody must have seen something,' Ames declared, fists so tightly clenched in his frustration that his fingernails were cutting into the palms of his hands. 'Somebody must know something.'

'Not I, Jimmy,' Rutherford said firmly. 'If I were you, I'd go and fetch the undertaker. Your papa needs his services rather than mine now. But there are others—a good many others, I may say—who do need me. So, if you'll excuse me, I'll be about my business.'

With lips compressed and a frown upon his brow, Ames made no reply but watched the doctor walk to the buggy that stood a few yards short of the scene, place his medical bag under the driving board, climb into his seat, pick up the reins, slap leather on hide, and set off along the street behind his trotting black. No doubt it had been all in the day's work to him, and Ames found himself shuddering in the sudden awareness that there was no aspect of human affairs so grim that it did not constitute the familiarity behind somebody's contempt.

'You just received some good advice,' a voice from the background said.

Ames craned, seeking out the speaker from among the watchers present with a cold eye. 'What was that, Vestry?'

'I heard Doc Rutherford advise you to fetch the undertaker.'

Nodding slowly, Ames held his ground for perhaps a moment too long.

'He'll still be lying there when you get back, Ames,' Vestry observed sardonically.

Incensed beyond the bearing, Ames faced round. He walked towards the speaker, and the folk covering the man opened up to provide a clear path. Then, as he moved into range, Ames let fly with an uppercut that detonated under the point of Vestry's jaw. Vestry toppled backwards into a heap and lay dazedly spitting and spluttering. A look of almost childish resentment came over his features as he asked thickly: 'What was that for?'

'You work it out yourself,' Ames responded stonily, then made a left turn and strode off up the street in the direction of the rather tumbledown carpenter's shop which, after returning from a business trip to New York City about two years ago—where the title had recently been coined—Billy Logan, the Brayton undertaker, had started calling his funeral parlour.

In fact the vainglorious Billy, a wizened little man clad in a white apron and green eyeshade, was awaiting Ames's arrival at his shop door. That he had heard the killer shot was beyond question, and that he had since been keeping himself informed of the further developments on the street, by a little judicious spying round the edge of the door jamb, was also beyond doubt. 'Well, you could have brought your barrow along,' Ames commented a trifle reproachfully.

Billy Logan dry-washed his hands and stood bent in false humility. 'Would that have been seemly, sir?'

'Who'd have given a damn?'

'Your pa was a fine man,' Logan

30

grieved. 'His death is a great loss to our community.'

'That wasn't quite what you said on the day that he asked you to reduce the price of town funerals,' Ames reminded bitterly.

'He's dead now, sir.'

'Yes, that makes all the difference, doesn't it?' Ames acknowledged. 'Over and done with; no future deed to take into account. You're a damned hypocrite, Billy—just like all the rest of them. Well, you'll get your full price on this job, and whatever extra you see fit to add. Because I want it done properly—from the first offices to the last turf on the grave.'

'Nothing but my best, sir.'

'Go on out the back and get your barrow,' Ames ordered. 'Is your man in today?'

'He's gathering apples.'

'Then I'll help you pick the body up.'

Billy Logan inclined his head and, turning away, scuttled through to the rear of his premises, while Ames stood horrified at some aspects of the dialogue that had gone before. Men said peculiar things in the stress of the moment, and past resentments surged out of nowhere—if only to taint the memory—but the spoken truth was less ugly than that which the mind harboured in silence. Ames figured that he had done the little he could to eliminate Billy Logan's humbug with a dose of truth and justice—since he didn't like the idea of his father's remains being handled by a mealy-mouthed enemy—but he guessed none of it mattered all that much, and went silently to join Logan as the undertaker emerged from the opening on the left of his premises, pushing a barrow before him.

Ames moved beside the cart as Logan walked it down the street, and they came in less than half a minute to the body and those who were still watching it. Logan halted the barrow at the best spot, then made some show of rolling up his sleeves. Ames waited for the man to complete this preparation; then, steeling himself, for there seemed something strange—and even vaguely abnormal about what he was doing—Ames got his hands under his dead parent's shoulders and lifted powerfully while Logan did the same at the sheriff's feet. It was all done in a moment or two, and Hank Ames lay slack-limbed and empty-faced upon the barrow, everything about him appearing displaced and unnatural; and his son averted his eyes as Billy Logan manoeuvred through a turn and then went trundling back up the street, he and his cart forming an incongruous sight that could as well have been operating in fun as earnest. Thirty paces more and the undertaker and his conveyance had passed from view; and Ames was abruptly conscious of Claude Vestry glowering at him and tenderly fingering a swollen chin. 'I left three-parts of a bottle in there,' Ames said, nodding at Johnson's Bar. 'Go and finish it.'

With neither word nor gesture, Vestry screwed round on his heel and stalked back into the saloon, while the other folk present broke up and drifted away now that the body had been removed and the drama gone out of things. Indeed, within a minute or so Ames was standing alone on an empty street and again considering the Hillwood Stage and Freight Office, where he was sure that a drape—this one hanging at a window which actually overlooked the main—had once more stirred. Laurel? Most likely. She would have to keep her nose in matters. Yet could this sly avoidance of him mean more than he had earlier suspected? Was it possible that she had kept dark because she had known what was about to happen? He was full of strange feelings which had to do with his father's murder. And not just as Laurel had impinged on the business, for Claude Vestry's behaviour had been peculiar too. The way the man—so much more the past enemy than the present friend—had intruded on his privacy as a perhaps deliberately diverting presence. There had been the trip also. He would still swear it had been done on purpose. Why? How about to keep him off the street for long enough after the shot had been fired to give the bushwhacker the time necessary to disappear completely? The answer met the question marks; since, on looking back to the gunshot, Ames was convinced that the bullet which had killed his father had been fired from a high position—from a nearby rooftop indeed—and it went without saying that a man clambering about on the tiles, while better placed for a shooting, had to be slower and more careful than one working at ground level.

Yes, he could see the objections. It was all too loose and improbable—possibly the product of a distraught mind—but his father was dead, and some kind of logical

34

situation must have embraced the murder. Recalling the position of the wound in the sheriff's chest, Ames narrowed his eyes and calculated the line down which the fatal slug had most probably flown, deciding almost at once that the rifleman had been positioned as like as not behind the parapet under the highest of the east-facing dormers at the top of the Moosegate hotel, which was the tallest building of any kind in town, and also a whorehouse that he knew Fanny Beales—the prettiest madam in the business and a long-time friend of Rex Mills—to dominate from her room up there.

Ames felt a strong urge to investigate the parapet above. But he had no authority to enter the hotel and approach the raised brickwork by a legitimate route. In fact when it came to playing the detective, he had no more rights as the son of the deceased than any other bystander. And if he asked for permission to examine the parapet, he was sure that the hotel would either flatly deny him or have him thrown out neck-and-crop; so it would be wise to either forgo his suspicions—at least until Deputy Sheriff Frank Broom got back to town—or give the doubtful area up there the once over by an illegal path. As he saw it in his mind's-eye, the latter would involve climbing the framework of the balconies that served the rising floors of the Moosegate until he reached the walk that the brickwork beneath the top window enclosed. It appeared a mildly dangerous undertaking, but not more than that, and he felt inclined to risk it; for this was a day when nothing any longer seemed to matter. If he broke his neck, nobody would care very much; but, if he pulled it off, he had the feeling that he might later have something to tell Frank Broom that the deputy could find interesting.

Disregarding any eyes that might be watching him from behind glass, Ames walked straight over to the hotel, moved into the alley on its eastern side, and decided there and then that he would be best served in his climb by the portion of the outer framework that was immediately before him, since this was formed by parallel timbers which rose from the ground to the northern corner of the parapet itself and had crosses of oak built into the twin uprights to provide additional integrity. Indeed, viewed from close up, the structure had plenty in common with a ladder, and he was now sure that he would come to no harm providing he watched out for signs of wear-and-tear and any hurt that ill-disposed human beings might try to do him.

Ames approached the uprights. Gripping them with his hands, he began to climb. The stretches required of his arms and legs were long ones—and his insteps frequently got pinched in the crosspoints of the oaken X's—but there was even less to the ascent than he had at first imagined, and his climb carried him upwards at an even pace which soon brought him towards the top of the hotel. He had heard nothing at any stage from inside the building, and no face had appeared at any of the numerous windows that overlooked his route towards the roof, and he arrived under the northern end of the parapet breathing a trifle heavily but otherwise without stress. After that it was the work of a minute only to reach up and grab the top of the brickwork with both hands, heave himself aloft by the strength of his arms, cock a leg over the parapet, roll inwards until he could set his guiding foot on the masonry which the raised brickwork enclosed, and finally come erect near the big dormer window that he had recently been contemplating from the ground.

He began to look around him, going down on his hands and knees to be thorough about it, but there was nothing on the thin surface mortar present to show that anybody had recently stood or crouched upon it while sighting a rifle. He worked the enclosed area over from end to end, crawling up and down parallel strips of the lichen-greened surface beneath him, but still came upon no sign that the killer had been up here; and he might well have left it at that and climbed back to the ground a disappointed man; but then, as a sort of sealing tribute to the care that he had exercised, he moved to the piece of wall below the dormer, seeking any marks that could have been made by bootsoles scrabbling there. Again he detected no telltale traces, and thought that he really must give it up now, when he saw a narrow slot with ragged edges that had been formed between the receding line of the mortar and the brickwork of the wall adjoining. This was in itself a discovery of no great importance, but it took on significance when Ames glimpsed a metallic object shining dully at a depressed angle within it and, using his right forefinger, he slowly prised what proved to be the case of a brass cartridge from it.

He sniffed at the shell's slightly blackened open end. It reeked of a recently fired charge. There could be little doubt that he had found the remains of the bullet which had slain his father. He rolled the case over and over in the palm of his left hand. One thing here was certain. This bullet had not been fired from a repeating rifle. It was too big for that, and could only have been discharged by a Springfield-Allin rifle, a single-shot breech-loading weapon which had been on standard issue throughout the infantry regiments of the United States Army for many years. A gun of the greatest reliability, it was also extremely accurate, and there were still plenty of men about who used it for target-shooting in preference to any of the various makes of repeating rifles which had proliferated the West ever since the days of the Civil War.

While Ames imagined that there would be other rifles of the make to be found in the district, he knew of only one Springfield-Allin in Bayton itself, and that was owned by Rex Mills, who had won a number of shooting contests with it in years gone by. Threads came together in his mind. There was something taking shape here. Mills' name was like a magnet that seemed to be attracting dubious happenings to it. First the man had been named as the seducer of Ames's girl. Then his moniker had come up in an obscure connection that was probably illegal. Add to that Laurel Bergen's peculiar behaviour and Claude Vestry's too familiar attitude—still keeping the original name in mind—and bring in a final reminder that Rex Mills and the woman who occupied the room behind the dormer had been thick ever since Mills had been old enough to start bedding females, and you had the possible ingredients for a plot to murder Sheriff Hank Ames with a shot from the parapet adjacent. That the sheriff's son had happened to wander into the doings at just the wrong moment had been purely coincidental. Yet even so, allowing that Mills had brought out his Springfield-Allin and gunned Hank Ames down, there would have been some good reason for it beyond the wish to kill; and, though the bushwhacking itself might not be instantly provable, it was not inconceivable that it could be brought home to Mills by getting him for his other likely wrongdoings first. Between this cartridge case and what Frank Broom probably knew about the suspect that he did not, Ames felt that the interested parties could already be some way towards avenging what had happened to his father. The details might seem a little involved for the time being, but they would become clearer as they were isolated and understood.

Intending to shin back to the ground at once, Ames began straightening up, but the crown of his head made sudden and painful contact with a solid object. Staggering backwards from the force of the impact, Ames perceived that the window above him had been silently opened while he was crouching over the slot into which the brass shell had either been hastily dropped or kicked. His presence had clearly been discovered, for Fanny Beales, elegant in blue silk and lace flounces—but hard-mouthed and cold-eyed for all that—was standing opposite him in the room behind the dormer with a Winchester rifle cocked and levelled in her hands. 'You filthy beast!' she spat at him. 'Get yourself in here this instant!'

Ames glanced swiftly towards the end of the parapet on his right, weighing his chances of getting away, but he realized that the risk wasn't worth it. He was guilty of no great offence, but Fanny could be relied upon to shoot straight if she had to. There was nothing he could do save obey; so, sliding the fired cartridge into a trouser-pocket, he grabbed the dormer's sill and began to climb.

THREE

Pulling himself completely through the window-space, Ames balanced for a moment on the inner sill; then he sprang to the floor beyond and drew himself erect before Fanny Beales, folding his arms as he met her apparently outraged gaze inquiringly. 'Tut, tut,' he murmured.

'You should be ashamed of yourself!' the madam declared.

'What for?' he demanded.

'You're a filthy Peeping Tom, Jimmy Ames, that's why!'

'Girl, you know better than that,' Ames

returned quietly. 'You know what I climbed up here for.'

'You wanted to peep in and see me in the buff!' she declared.

'And that would be something new?'

'New? What are you talking about?'

'For you to be seen in the buff,' Ames said, tongue in cheek. 'Most guys in town have seen you so. Trade necessity, as you might say.'

'You cheeky—!'

'One of my many failings,' Ames sighed, wincing as the Winchester's trigger gave visibly under the pressure of her finger. 'Watch what you're doing with that rifle, Fanny! It damn nigh went off then!'

'Nobody would blame me for killing a Peeping Tom!'

'Maybe not,' Ames conceded. 'You sell your charms, Fanny—and there are other things about you that I'm not struck on—but I'd believed you a woman of conscience until now.'

'So what's changed it?'

'You stood by and let Rex Mills murder my pa.'

The woman paled, visibly so, despite the powder that covered her face, and the rouge upon her cheeks stood out

43

unnaturally. 'You don't know what you're saying, Jimmy Ames!'

'Oh, yes I do, Fanny,' he said, letting a note of sympathy creep into his voice. 'Needs must? Was that it? That one can be a prize bastard when he likes! He wouldn't think twice about busting your nose and scarring your lips. Sure, it's a hard old world, and you have to get your living!'

'Lord a'mercy!' Fanny Beales scoffed. 'How you do run on, sonny! I knew your pa had been killed, yes—one of the bell-boys ran up here and told me that—but I'm short on the details beyond that.'

Ames decided to push it for all he was worth; and he drew the brass cartridge case out of his pocket and held it towards her in the palm of his right hand. 'I found it under your window, Fanny. I suspect Rex dropped it in his haste, made to pick it up, and ended by kicking it into that crack which runs between the edge of the mortar out there and the wall.'

'It's only a brass shell!' the woman announced contemptuously. 'I once saw a battlefield littered with them!'

'Who are you trying to kid?' Ames scorned. 'Have a sniff at it, honey!'

'Get that dirty thing away from me!' she

warned, snatching back her head as far as it would go. 'I don't know how it got out there and—and that's the truth.'

'And—and that's a lie,' Ames mocked anew. 'Let me put a quick end to this trouble, Fanny. All you have to do is tell me that Rex Mills was up here and fired down at my father. If you say it was force-work, I'll stand by you up to the hilt. I don't want to hurt you. It's Rex Mills I want to fix.'

'Are you out of your mind?' the woman asked soberly. 'You know very well how it is between Rex and me. Besides, you've got it completely wrong—there's nothing to tell. It's all in your head, Jim. Sheer imagination. You've been away since goodness knows when man! What can you know? What could you know in those circumstances.'

'I know enough,' Ames insisted. 'I've already heard the right people talk. And it all fits. You must be aware that Rex Mills is tripping the fandango with Laurel Bergen. He's not worth any kind of loyalty from you.'

'Oh, so that's it!' Fanny Beales exclaimed, her expression suggesting that she had just been enormously enlightened.

'You want to get poor Rex hanged in the hope Laury Bergen will then come blubbering to you. Think again, Jim! You don't understand women. Sugar and spice and all things nice, eh? Women have different shapes, but they're not so different from men when they're looking for partners. I meet Laury Bergen every day of my life. If it wasn't Rex with her, it would be some other handsome varmint who tickled her fancy. I don't think about Rex when he isn't with me, and you shouldn't think about Laury.'

'Where's that Springfield-Allin of his?' Ames asked abruptly, going off at a tangent. 'It occurs to me that you have it hidden somewhere up here. He'd never have dared carry it back outside after shooting pa with it. Such a gun is too conspicuous.'

'I've had enough of this,' Fanny Beales said. 'I caught you fair and square outside my window, and I'm going to hand you over to the law.'

'What law?' Ames demanded bitterly. 'The law's lying dead in Billy Logan's shed, and Deputy Sheriff Broom is out of town. Best cry quits, Fanny. Don't try to hang on to me. You can't tell how

46

Rex Mills might take it anyway. What's more, wouldn't playing jailor clash with the other things you have to do?' He lifted an eyebrow, his cynicism shifting its track a little. 'Always supposing you had such an idea.'

Her brow knitted, Fanny Beales chewed it over with herself, her expression changing slightly as her mind moved among the various aspects of the matter. Then she gave her chin a jerk that was curt and almost masculine, indicating the window with the muzzle of her rifle. 'Go—by the way you came!' she ordered.

'Can't you let me walk down through the hotel?' he asked innocently.

'Go to blazes!' she advised. 'I know the questions you'd be asking.'

'They'll still be there to ask,' he reminded her. 'So they do worry you, then? They shouldn't, not with all that innocence about.'

'Get out of here, Jimmy!'

Shrugging, Ames faced round and returned to the window, climbing out of it feet first and making the brief slide back to the mortar-covered floor beneath it.

'You won't ask,' Fanny Beales said from behind him, the note of confidence in her voice faintly jeering.

He didn't glance back but went straight to the northern end of the parapet. No, he thought, as he swung himself over the brickwork and groped around with his feet until he had his soles firmly fixed on the framework which led to the ground, he wouldn't be asking. He'd still get no further than the hotel desk—which, in a sense, brought him back to where he'd started—and he doubted that he'd learn much by waylaying individuals. For the word must have gone round by this time that the members of the hotel staff were to say nothing if private questions were asked concerning the sheriff's murder, and it would be very difficult to isolate the right people anyhow, since the Moosegate employed a fair number.

Ames climbed as smoothly down the connecting balcony frames as he had climbed up them. He reached the ground without incident. Then, still more than a little shaken by the general run of events, he made his way home; and, retrieving the key from under the step, unlocked the front door and stepped into the hall, aware, as he closed up behind him, of the distinctive smells of tobacco and boot polish which had always identified his father's presence for him. It was hard to credit that Hank Ames was dead, and that the sheriff's place would see him no more. The sensation was a weird one, and it hammered home the fact of death through the silence of the house as nothing else could have done. Ames felt a moment of paralysing grief, and a sob choked in his throat, but he took an instant grip on himself in the knowledge that nothing robbed a man's energies like any form of strong emotion. His father had departed—as his mother had departed a year or two back—and he was left here. The things that had been theirs were now his. Nature required that he live out his life in his time, as his parents had lived out theirs in an earlier day. He must keep calm until after pa's funeral. Then he could pipe his eye a little if he still needed to and make his decisions. There was a good home here, but a bigger and more attractive life in Cheyenne. Yes, he could be comfortable in Brayton and find himself work that paid well enough. Security would no longer be a problem. But he was too young to settle for comfort and security. There was Laurel too. Yet she might still prove part of memories that he would prefer to forget. Nothing was exactly clear cut, but when was it ever?

He walked upstairs and entered his bedroom. A faint smell of mothballs met him. The room had been spotlessly kept in his absence, and the bed linen was white as snow. Regardless of that, he kicked off his boots and stretched out on the counterpane, thoughts of Laurel Bergen at once returning and soon ousting all from his mind. He must find out how he stood with the girl; the business had reduced itself to that for now. What he needed was a long, quiet talk with her, and a relaxed atmosphere would be vital for that. Ought he to invite her here? Or should he go round to her home this evening? He figured the latter the more correct course, unless she wished it otherwise, and he reckoned that he would let the working day spin itself out before he left the house again.

Presently he slept. He awoke to a changed atmosphere. The heat of the earlier day had gone. This was September after all. He got up with the shivers in his flesh, and his eyes were affronted by the near darkness which hung outside his window. Then his stomach rolled, reminding him that he had not eaten since a scanty breakfast taken on the trail, and he thought of his horse also—which he had left tied at the nearest hitching rail a short distance down the street. The brute must be hungry too, and he decided that later on he would put it into the livery barn, where it would get proper care and attention until he had made up his mind what he was going to use it for next. The fact was, he supposed, the critter was one of the more pampered kind. A bank guard didn't do that much riding as a rule, and his bay stallion had become more of a leisure mount than anything else. But all that was of little importance. This business with Laurel remained what mattered for now.

He walked downstairs, yawning hugely and rubbing at his eyes. Going to the lamp which stood on the hall table near the foot of the stairs, he struck a match and touched off the wick. Then he carried his light along to the pantry and set it on the sill behind the window. Now he scooped a mug of water out of the drinking bucket and, with his thirst slaked, went on to open the tin that had always contained the shortcakes. Helping himself to a couple of the chunky pastries, he stood and ate

51

until his hunger was stemmed; and then he picked up the lamp again and passed into the kitchen, where he combed his hair and shrugged off the knowledge that he needed a shave, reckoning that he wouldn't get close enough to Laury for it to matter anyhow. After that he left the house, locking up and hiding the key in the same place as before.

Now he strode westwards up the main street. The older part of Brayton was located in that direction, and Laurel Bergen lived out there, right on the edge of town, in one of the first permanent dwellings that had ever been erected in this district. As he moved along, oily lights glowed in the windows on either hand, splashing the ground with their reflections, and he was conscious of the lunar crescent over to his left struggling with a run of low, dark cloud. The night had a clammy, blowy feeling about it as what could be a rain wind lifted fitfully and moaned the same in the southwest. Wyoming was a green place—the most green and beautiful in the whole of the West—but the greenness depended on rain, and when it started to rain in these parts, as it invariably did around this time in the early fall, it didn't know when to leave off. Ames prayed that it wasn't going to start raining tonight. Sunshine prospered uncertain love-suits, but the rain made women contrary and put mildew into everything.

Ames neared Laurel's home. He drew a deep breath to steady the throbbing of his heart and quell the churning of his stomach. He ached to see Laurel, yet feared the sight of her face. She held his future in her hands, and undoubtedly knew it. The eternal female, she could be downright stony when she wanted—wordless, at best tactless, often an unfeeling little miss—joying, indeed, in the power that her beauty gave her over men. She had, figuratively speaking, kicked the guts out of him a time or two before today, and he had a presentiment that it was about to happen again and was daunted. Maybe he ought to go back home and leave things as they were for tonight. Tomorrow was another day. Tomorrow Laury might be another girl. He, too, might be a little different.

No! This had to be done. A day more or less wasn't going to alter anything much. This had to be faced; he must grasp the nettle and refuse to be a moral coward. If Miss Bergen's favour ran too deeply

53

elsewhere, he must accept it—go and get drunk, spend a hectic night with one of Fanny Beales's floozies, or blow his brains out; do something other than agonize in a manner unbefitting his mother's son.

There was the girl before him! But she had her back to him and had not seen him as yet. She had just led her horse out of the gate at the further end of her father's property and mounted up—silhouettes all—and he watched her point the creature westwards and raise her quirt to goad it into motion.

Ames opened his mouth to call to her; then shut it once more. He could not quite say why. The heavy airs drew sweat to his brow, and the dark horizon again moaned softly. What the dickens could a young woman be going out at this time of the evening for? There was nothing much west of here but the wilderness. Exercise? Perhaps. Laury knew all about looking after her figure. But the night and the atmosphere were hardly congenial to riding alone. Especially when one was reasonably gregarious, as was the case with Laury. So everything pointed to an assignation. Fine. But you didn't go up to the woods to make love on a blowy September night with little moon and not a star in sight. It appeared then that she was going to meet somebody about business that was unconcerned with kisses and sweet nothings; and his mind flew back to that last lecture from his father and what Hank Ames had said about Laurel Bergen's need for a bad shock to put her thinking straight. Could Rex Mills also be involved in the girl's life at a level other than the amatory one? If he was, Laury could be involved in actual wrongdoing. Crime related to both the sheriff's death and his lecturing. The linkage and reasoning were definitely there, if once more a trifle vague.

Watching as the girl and her horse began fading into the gloom before him, Ames realized that it still wasn't too late for him to shout after her, and he wanted to do so, but still something within himself—that possessed a hint of vindictiveness—would not let him. He wanted to follow Laury, but did he have the right? Of course he didn't—unless there was skulduggery involved; but how could he be sure about that if he didn't pursue? Oh, what the hell! Did he have to be so precise? Right or wrong, he was going to ride after that blasted female! If he was wrong, he'd make sure she never learned of his deceit; but if he proved right—Well, he would be right, and that would make everything right.

Facing about, Ames ran back down the main street to the rail at which his horse was still secured. Freeing the brute, he yanked its head to the left and stepped up, kneeing for a trot, and the horse carried him up the middle of the beaten way and out of town. Here, stirring his sluggish mount with the rowels, he clapped on a bit of pace, for though the trail ran straight ahead for the next four miles without coming to any form of junction—which meant that he should have plenty of ground in the normal way over which to regain contact with Laurel Bergen—there was, of course, always the slight chance that she would turn off into the surrounding country at some unexpected point and so completely lose herself to him that all his scheming would be brought to nothing.

After travelling really fast for an uneasy mile or so, Ames drew his mount down to a steady canter and began to peer ahead a little anxiously, seeking any flicker of sparks or glimpse of person which might warn that he had done all the catching up immediately necessary, but he saw nothing in the mingled fields of sepia and black before him and felt a new tension grip his throat as he feared that he might already have overrun his purpose and betrayed himself by sound, for the irons certainly rang on this flint-studded track.

Putting more pressure on the bit, Ames hung back; and then he stopped altogether, listening intently. He had been hoping the clouds would roll away, letting what moon there was ride clear and shine down unveiled, but instead the rack thickened and the occasional bluster of the wind became a steady booming swirl. There was rain coming all right. Rely on the weather to break as soon as he left Cheyenne! Where was that girl? His judgement of these things was usually pretty good. She shouldn't be all that far away.

He resumed forward motion. The night closed in, winding itself about him like a sheet of blackness. The atmosphere chilled, and a few drops of rain spattered on his face. Then the sky split and white lightning flared out of it, forking and running, and hill and plain were illuminated by a moment of day. Ames saw the trail thrusting westwards, and Laurel Bergen trotting forward about a quarter of a mile ahead of him. He relaxed again, for he had certainly never been within earshot of the girl, and there had been nothing in her posture to suggest that she had any interest in her backtrail whatsoever. Everything about her pointed to this being a routine ride and, as the lightning again forked vividly—this time bringing with it tremendous peals of thunder—he wondered in a moment of sobering clarity whether he had ever really known Laury at all. Perhaps he had only seen in the girl what he had wanted to see, and that was where he had made his great mistake.

The rain held off a minute longer, but it had to come. When it did, it fell from the sky like water from a bucket turned upside down. One moment Ames was dry, but the next he was soaked to the skin. The biting chill of it made him shiver, and he felt an answering tremble from the horse beneath him. Suddenly sheet lightning glared behind the clouds, its already shielded glow hardly penetrating the rain, and all that was visible of the surrounding landscape could have been a vision of the ocean floor. The thunder rent and tore overhead, and its echoes cracked and boomed through the vault of heaven. Then new chains of fire jumped and flickered along the skylines, and a stink of ozone hung spent in streamers of mist which could be seen only while the lightning flashed. After that the storm blew out as quickly as it had arrived, and its last brilliant flare-up revealed the tightly hunched shape of Laurel Bergen as she pulled to the right, guiding her horse off the trail, and went climbing away into the black woods of the Medicine Bow.

Ames stuck to it. If the girl could take it, so could he. Easing his back inside his sodden shirt, he made the few mental notes he could. Rain was still slicing through the gloom, but part of the heavens had cleared and released the crescent moon from bondage. Now the white segment was shining against the departing stormclouds, and his eyes, accustomed to the blacker state which had gone before, found that they could make out the flooded surface of the trail beneath him and the shapes of the larger objects adjacent. His mind seemed to keep slipping cogs, and distance became harder to judge with every moment. He discovered that he no longer had any idea of where Laury had turned off and, reduced to guessing at the spot, drew his horse aside where the edge of the trail appeared to be broken. Trees loomed at him, and he moved into near total darkness again, a roof of pine boughs dripping upon him and the water-logged odour of the forest floor rising into his nostrils.

Within a minute or so, something like panic swept over him. What had he done? He was already lost and disorientated. A child would have known better than to enter the woods in these conditions. He ought to have thought more carefully before leaving the trail. Not for the first time in his life he had missed the obvious. He had allowed himself to be totally governed by the thought that Laury simply knew this area better than he, and that that covered everything. But he realized now that this could be true only up to a point. Even she would have required some kind of path or markers to follow in this darksome hour. Definite pointers must exist where she had turned off, and he, by failing to give any thought to looking for them, had left the beaten path too soon and was now wandering in the forest without even the instincts of a blind man to guide him. He judged that he would do well to stop about now, let his senses settle down, and await the coming of more clement weather before trying to pinpoint the direction of what must be the still not far distant trail and to attempt riding back to it. Since he accepted that he had lost all contact with Laury Bergen for tonight and now had no hope of following her to her goal.

A wall of unseen fir boughs suddenly resisted Ames's groping presence. He halted, happy to let the low-hanging barrier confirm his mind and, after he had sat there for about a minute, he was even more pleased that he had ceased all movement, for out of the trees to his left came the slow crashing of what his imagination told him was a horse that was being aimlessly ridden by a rider who was as fully lost in the forest as he was himself. Laury? It seemed likely.

Then this too was confirmed for him as a rather familiar male voice called the girl's name from not too far away to the east of him, and he heard her shout in answer: 'I'm over here, Rex! I'm—I'm lost!'

'Hang that for a yarn!' the male speaker shouted in response. 'Hold still, honey! Me and Joe will be with you shortly!'

Ames listened intently. The girl also had

ceased moving now. But Rex Mills and the man called Joe were highly audible as they came in from the right. Indeed, their course seemed to be bringing them straight at him. Yet what could he do but hold still and hope for the best?

FOUR

Ames felt a tightness in his chest. He realized that he was holding his breath more and more fixedly. The two men were still approaching what amounted to his hiding place on a bisecting line. He could hear their horses snuffling above the cracking of dead branches and the brushing of wet pine foliage against hide and clothing. Soon he judged that they would be upon him in seconds more, and his right hand went to his holster; but then the oncoming animals seemed to encounter another part of the natural barrier which had brought him to a stop, and he heard them sheer away slightly to their right. They finally passed his mount's nose at a distance of no more than two yards—and Ames was sure for a long moment that he must have been discovered—but nothing occurred to give substance to his fear, and the beasts moved on into the nearby growth with no obvious diminution of purpose.

'Laury!' Mills called again.

'Here!' she replied.

Ames breathed out, then sucked another quick breath. The meeting came in sounds of human relief, and a moment or two of equine snorting and prancing. The horses and people couldn't be more than ten yards from the listener now. 'We feared you might miss your path, honey,' Ames heard Rex Mills finally comment. 'She sure was a storm. We ain't had one like that in a day or two.'

'Nor yet a year,' an older male voice put in.

'You can thank Joe Fullwood that we came out here after you,' Rex Mills jested. 'I was all for leaving you to the goblins.'

'That's a fine thing to tell a girl!' Laury Bergen protested, half laughing. 'You really are a skunk, Rex!'

'Now I wonder why you love me?' Mills chuckled. 'Would you be a female skunk, honey?'

'Cut it out, Mills!' the man named Fullwood protested. 'That's no kind of talk!'

'He's got a yen for you, sweetheart!' Mills jeered. 'Fifty years old and still got a yen. The loins on him! May it be so with me.'

'So long as it's me you want,' the girl warned.

'Aw, you'll have had enough of me long since!' Mills declared dismissively. 'Ain't a thing to last, Laury! You'll be looking elsewhere come Thanksgiving!'

'Jim Ames *is* back in town.'

'Sure, honey, I saw him,' Mills said. 'Fanny Beales told me some more, We mustn't underestimate that long bastard. He's dangerous!'

'Could've been him we thought we saw riding behind her just now,' Fullwood commented.

'That's a thought, Joe,' Mills observed soberly. 'Blast me if it ain't! And it's no new thing, eh?'

'What are you saying?' Laury Bergen asked sharply. 'Tell me, Joe. Rex is so full of nonsense, I never know how much I can trust from him.'

'Oh, Rex and me were sitting real high

64

when the first of that lightning flashed,' Joe Fullwood explained. 'We were able to pick out your little shape across the treetops, and we thought we saw a rider shadowing you.'

'On a night like this!' the girl scoffed. 'Pop said it was coming, but I wouldn't listen to him. All the same, I wouldn't have left the house if I hadn't promised Rex. You two imagined that rider. You've been drinking whisky again. I can smell it on your lips, Rex.'

'All for the want of you!' he assured her. 'I'm seriously in the need, honey. There are two ways a woman can drive a man to drink!'

Laury laughed, the sound strange and almost musical amidst the dull dripping of the rain. 'Fool!'

'He's always got a bottle in his hand,' Fullwood said sternly. 'But I hadn't been drinking, Laury. There was a man behind you on the trail.'

'So,' the girl said. 'Folk travel all hours. You can get to Walcott this way.'

'In a day or two,' Fullwood agreed. 'It was you mentioned a night like this.'

'Are you criticising me, Joe?'

'Heaven forbid!' Fullwood protested.

'Does no harm to throw a glance back now and again,' Mills said, the banter gone from his voice and a note of grim seriousness now present. 'This is no childish sport, honey. It's a dangerous game we play. We'll last just as long as we watch what we're doing every moment of the day and night.'

'Now and again?' the girl asked touchily. 'Every moment? Do they correspond?'

'You know what I mean,' Mills snapped.

'Don't kick it out, Laury,' Fullwood warned—'don't kick it out!'

'Half the time you men don't speak the English language!' Laury declared.

'Miss High-and-Mighty!' Mills taunted. 'Sounds to me like you need a paddling. You're great while you're stuffing your purse. Can't do that all the time, y'know.'

'That's not true, Rex,' the girl said coldly. 'If you want me to say it, I will. I'm the most important person here. I provide the targets. Yes, I was followed once. I admit it—there! But I don't want any more killing. We've had sufficient of that already. You men are far too quick to make murder your solution.'

'Only when there's no other,' Mills grated. 'It's your dear little neck we've been saving too—and don't you forget it! You wouldn't be the first pretty girl to swing. No, sirree!'

'They couldn't hang me!' Laury bleated.

'Could and would,' Mills assured her. 'You're in line for it, honey—right behind old Joe and me. True, Joe?'

Fullwood was clearly not prepared to answer that one. 'Well, what have you got for us old bears, Laury?' he asked, both his heartiness and the sudden change of subject strained. 'My men are running to fat and wind on beans and rest!'

'Oh, don't ask me now,' the girl said, her quaver betraying that she was still shaken by the talk which had gone before. 'I'm wet through and chilled to the bone.'

Mills chuckled wickedly. 'There's a roaring fire in the cave, Laury, and I'll soon have you out of those wet things. If you need warming up some, I'm your man!'

'When you're not that old whore's,' Laury said fretfully.

'Fanny Beales!' Mills pooh-poohed. 'She's just the girl I used to know!'

'What a lie!' Laury scorned in deep and dreary exasperation. 'Take me to the cave—please!'

67

'Bet your boots, kid!' Fullwood answered sympathetically. 'She's right, Rex. What the hell are we about? We're letting this consarned forest drip down our necks when we could be in the warm and dry.'

'I'm not holding anybody up!' Mills protested innocently. 'Giddup!'

But before the unseen speakers could move off, the thing that the eavesdropping Ames least wished to happen occurred. There was a crashing noise over to the right as some big animal—most likely a deer—which had been lying low in the brush up to now suddenly spooked, and its flight through the darkened forest was all too traceable by the ear.

'Somebody there—god-dammit!' Rex Mills raged, and a sixgun set up a thunderous pulsing.

The bullets tore through the foliage within inches of Ames and his mount. Feeling his horse stiffen into what could be the start of a kick-up, Ames threw all his will behind the strength of his hands and the weight of his knees, holding the creature down; and the mount, seeming to understand the need for its continued immobility and silence, held firm, its ears detectably pricking as, at a shout from

Mills, the nearby trio wheeled through the undergrowth and started after the noises of flight which still echoed back to the secret listener from his right.

Ames again sensed the movement of his enemies directly before him. Cocking his head, he let the sounds of the chase recede. He wasn't certain as to whether he should follow the two men and the girl or not. It was probable that he would gain no advantage from it, and might even meet real trouble in the process, but curiosity forced him into motion and he fetched slowly round to the right, forcing his way through the unseen canopy of hanging fir that had earlier checked his wandering and coming to open space which freed him to progress in the wake of the riders ahead at a slow pace that he felt was nevertheless plenty fast enough.

It was a tight, stressful business—this pursuit by ear—and it made him sweat all over, despite the rain that soaked him; and the nervous tension was increased tenfold as a woman's scream, high, baffled, and terrified, seemed to swoop through the treetops and set his heart pounding. Reining back with some force, he lifted in his stirrups, promptly associating the cry with Laury Bergen and supposing that she had come to harm, but then he realized that the direction from which the scream had come struck squarely across the route taken by his enemies and had certainly originated at a distance from his present location that the other riders could not possibly have reached in the time. He thought of banshees, and then about men who heard things, but neither idea found much favour with him, and he was forced to conclude that there really was another female nearby and that she had just screamed piteously into the night for some reason that he might never know. Considered more closely, of course, the unknown woman almost certainly had something to do with the gang at whose presence nearby Joe Fullwood's talk had hinted, but that too was another mystery which would have to keep him guessing for now.

He went on listening in the direction from which the scream had come, wondering if it might repeat, but he heard nothing else to startle him and realized all at once that, in shifting his concentration so largely, he had almost lost contact with the other source of noise in the forest. He kneed his horse forward again, trying to fix the line of his renewed pursuit from the rumours of it remaining, but the faint sounds were too confused and infrequent to give him a true bearing and he now advanced by something little better than guesswork.

Ames became aware of drifting to his left. He made no attempt to alter this, and also found that he was climbing again. This rather aimless movement—dependent on tiny blurts of noise out of the more distant woods—covered his progress for the next half an hour, and it came as quite a surprise to him when he saw that he had cleared the upper treeline and was riding parallel with the foot of a considerable ridge that drew its jagged rimrock through the dim moonlight high above and sent what he judged to be its south-facing wall tumbling to meet the pinewoods in a series of slopes and ribbed precipices that made the whole appear unclimbable. He supposed that, on the evidence of what he had overheard, there must be an approachable cave somewhere along this stretch of stone, but he nevertheless wondered where it could be located. The ridge looked about as inhospitable as any that he had ever encounted.

His mind idling thus, Ames accepted that his follow up on Mills, Fullwood and Laury, had long ago lost all direction and purpose. They might be almost anywhere now, within a square mile or two, and were most likely making tracks for their hideout by this time. He was just dawdling around up here now and wondering how the dickens he could get back to the town trails before daylight. It hadn't really stopped raining yet, and the moon's sickle kept coming and going in the clouds, which meant that it would be as dark as ever down among the trees and that he would only lose his sense of direction again when he entered the lower forest. If he must suffer a night on the mountain, it might as well be up here—where he could see a little—as down there where he would be able to see virtually nothing.

Then a faint sound of iron striking rock reached him from ahead and slightly below. His mind quickened instantly, and tension knotted itself anew into his vitals. He peered hard down the right side of his mount's neck. Movement tremored in his eye. Again shock had come along to brace a low ebb. The trio from the forest depths had obviously circled upwards and were now riding the reciprocal of his own track eastwards; and it occurred to him that, if he had spotted them in the dim visibility of the dip before him, they could the more easily have picked him out against the lesser obscurity of the rock up here. But there had been no alarm, so he had to assume that the riders below were tired and no longer paying the attention they should. Thus he drifted quietly to his right and let his course settle towards the upper limit of the trees, and within a minute he had re-entered the forest and was drawing rein in the blackest of the shadows at its edge, eyes turned upwards as he gazed towards the natural path at the base of the ridge and the trio of almost spectral riders who were now entering his field of vision from the right. The three became audibly vocal as they climbed. 'I'd have staked my last dollar I saw something,' Ames heard Rex Mills say, the man's voice querulously challenging. 'It sure as hell looked like a horseman to me, Joe!'

'God-dammit-to-hell, boy!' Fullwood's pleading tones protested. 'Ain't you sick of it yet? You're deceiving yourself! You did it before—over that bolting animal back there.'

'We don't know that for sure,' Mills responded obstinately. 'I reckon we ought to nose down there on the left and have a look.'

'No!' Fullwood answered decisively. 'I've had enough of those trees for one night, mister. What I want's to get back to the cave and find out how come Arnie Jacobs let that girl let out the squawk she did. I'll skin him with a blunt knife if he got careless!'

'It's what he became!' Laury Bergen's voice averred petulantly. 'Rex, I'm still wet through. I want to get dry!'

'Would you rather get hung?' Mills demanded.

'We've been over that,' Fullwood cut in impatiently. 'Enough's enough, boy! Let's keep going. You don't want your girl to catch cold, do you?'

'Aw, she's tougher than you and me put together, Joe!' Mills flung back unfeelingly. 'I'm going down to have a look-see. You two ride on.'

'All right!' Fullwood snapped. 'But don't expect me to send back for you if you go missing!'

74

'Tain't so likely!' Mills scorned.

Ames had a faint impression of the man breaking away from his companions and starting downwards in the direction of the forest. He waited to see no more, but turned his back on the descending rider and kneed his own horse deeper into the pinewood. An ear tilted over his shoulder, he traced Mills' rather noisy line of descent and judged that the man was still acting on suspicion rather than any kind of certainty, and he reckoned that if the worst did come to the worst and the other should detect some rumour of his presence, he would still be able to avoid contact with his hunter by the simple expedient of varying his direction in the kind of intermittent fashion which the darkness amidst the trees would make all the more baffling.

Thus Ames continued his slow ride towards the forest's heart confidently enough and, as the minutes went by, he perceived that the slightly hesitant noises of the searcher in his wake were growing fainter and fainter, and before long he felt a certainty within himself that Mills had abandoned his random quest and was now returning to the ridge above. So all was well. He had once more eluded his enemies, and again left them guessing as to whether he was there or not.

It was indeed all very satisfactory. Ames took his mind off what he was doing to give himself a metaphorical pat on the back. This was not very wise in his present circumstances, for his horse gave a small warning snort and, misinterpreting the sound, he forced the creature on when he ought to have let it halt. Suddenly the mount's fore-hooves went sliding over what seemed to be terraced earth. Now the brute pitched to the right, throwing its rider from it, and Ames found himself rolling downhill at an increasingly rapid pace. His body bumped against this and bounced off that, crushing undergrowth between times, and his senses whirled and fiery lights flashed inside his skull. He fought to check himself but realized in a moment of panic that he had no power at all over what was happening to him. He had become the victim of his own weight and intensifying gravity. Down he went and down, and was close to blacking out from the spinning motion alone, when he came by a terrific blow on the head. His senses fragmented and seemed to fly apart. There was a last split second of awareness, and then darkness welled up and wiped out his consciousness—and it seemed to him that he would go on spinning downhill through the forest for all eternity.

There was grey light around him when he came to himself and opened his eyes. He realized almost at once that he was lying belly down with his chin drooping forward into a position that was unsupported and lower than the rest of him. Space yawned under his face—and it seemed to him that he could feel the chill of water rising to meet his flesh—but his eyes refused to focus and reveal to him what this was about.

Then Ames felt a terrible aching in his head. Never had he been afflicted by such pain before. Nor was that the whole of it, since he hurt everywhere that a joint or muscle could hurt, and the agony made him vomit bile—which splashed into the water that he had previously sensed below him and could now begin to see. For, while his body was stretched out upon the bank, his head hung over the edge of a woodland pond which was not all that large but gave the impressions of being very deep. Now it occurred to Ames that his eye was meeting another, and that this one was opaque and dead and set in the head of a bloated roan horse which was floating just beneath the surface of the pond, its reins writhing sluggishly in the wind-stirred liquid and its stirrups also riding the green water in a semi-buoyant fashion.

His brain still muddled, Ames supposed dully that the dead horse must be his own and, though he knew there was something wrong with the thought, a minute went by before he realized what it was. The colour wasn't the right one. His stallion was a bay, more yellow than red, but the defunct mount was sort of bluish and covered in white hair. Whose horse was it? Damned if he knew—or much cared just then. Where was his own? He felt it necessary to find the critter fast, since he wouldn't get far without it. Could he get up? He fought to gather his limbs and stand erect, knowing that this was the crucial test. Yes. He rose to his feet and held more or less steady. Amazing as it seemed—in the light of returning memories of his tumble—nothing appeared to be broken. Sure, he seemed to have aged about fifty years while he had lain unconscious, but he hoped that would reverse itself in the course of the day ahead. And, hardly able to credit the major fact of his survival—which was that if he had skidded an extra yard off the slope behind him, he would have plunged into the pond and drowned—he staggered a full circle at the water's-edge, and finally caught sight of his horse off to the right of him, where it stood, bedraggled and drooping, beside a heap of boulders.

Shivering, Ames felt at his garments. They had been soaked before his accident, and were still utterly sodden. It was obvious that he had lain unconscious for most of the night, and now seemed equally clear that he had been further rained on during a large part of the time. He would be lucky if he didn't catch his death of cold—though he often wondered about people and their harping on such things; for he had been drenched a hundred times during the cattle drives of his teens and never taken the slightest harm. There was a whole lot more to taking cold than folk would have you believe. But he was mighty uncomfortable all the same, and would be glad to get home and make a change of clothing.

He moved towards his horse, and the animal backed away from him a yard or so, favouring its right pastern. Frowning, he caught up with the brute and knelt beside it, fearing that it might have sustained a fracture at that one weak point where even the best horse doctor could do little to repair the damage, and his hand went instinctively towards his Colt—which he found still securely thonged into its holster—but a close glance at the suspect hoof told him that there was no break and that the brute, like its master, was no worse than still sore and shaken from its tumble. They had been a lucky pair, but he would have to be careful of the horse even so, for he was no expert and there could still be more wrong with the creature than met the eye.

Straightening up again, Ames felt a slight giddiness. He breathed deeply to eliminate this short-lived disability. Then he let his gaze travel slowly around the stone pot in the forest floor which contained the pond, and he was suddenly aware of movement ahead of him and on his right—a short way up the tree-denuded slope, indeed, which angled back for fifty yards or so to the west of this place before the omnipresent pinewood took over again. Again Ames peered intently—though satisfied that no human agency was present—and he made out a big coyote scraping away vigorously at a sandy spot on the incline, which was heavily dotted with lichen-covered rocks, clumps of bramble, and other forms of undergrowth that had the capacity to root where the earth was loose and thin.

The rough, dog-like brute seemed unaware of Ames's presence—and wholly involved with some probably carrion discovery that it had made—and, clapping his hands to set it fleeing, the watching man left his horse and angled up the acclivity to where the coyote had been scraping at the soil. He came upon an outlined slot at the bottom of a water channel, which had plainly been doing great drainage work all night long, and saw there the kind of sinkage which suggested a shallow burial. Squatting again, he imitated the coyote and began clawing back the dirt from the end of the slight subsidence on his right, and he had not removed more than six inches of the wet soil there when a man's face came into view and he knew instinctively that he had stumbled upon evidence of murder.

FIVE

With his own aches and pains forgotten, and working at speed now, Ames uncovered the whole upper body of the corpse and used his own neckerchief to clean the deceased's face. He didn't recognize the features—which were those of a youngish man and rather handsome in a rough-hewn sort of way—but the deputy sheriff's badge on the fellow's shirt was identification enough. This poor guy must have been Frank Broom, his pa's assistant—the man sent out to do that unspecified investigation job in the Medicine Bow—and, like Hank Ames, he had been shot through the heart. This looked like another crime committed by Rex Mills and company, and it meant that whatever had been known against the crooks by the local law was now the secret forever of dead brains. There would be no help for Jim Ames from the deputy sheriff; and, if the said Jim went on trying to avenge his father, he would have to expand on whatever he had already learned for himself and ride even further into harm's way. It would be foolish to wait for some newcomer to the office of sheriff to start over on this case. The effort might well have to travel cold trails, and that in itself would lead to almost certain failure. Even a gifted detective needed to catch a case in full flood in order to pick up the spirit of what was taking place.

Ames fully covered the dead man again. It was unthinkable right now that he should completely disinter the corpse and take it home with him. Broom had been dead and buried long enough for decomposition to have started, and Ames didn't fancy either soiling his saddle or giving the air the chance to take the dissolution process a step further on the way back to town. Billy Logan would have to make the necessary arrangements to pick up the remains. Death was his occupation after all, and it would certainly be his job to carry out Frank Broom's funeral.

Returning to his horse, Ames decided against mounting up. The forest floor was too rough hereabouts to risk that hurt pastern to a perhaps serious stumble. He would find out whether the animal could still carry him when they had put the pinewood behind them. That shouldn't take long. The difficulty of finding the right direction through the trees no longer existed. He could now see well enough to take full advantage of the downgrade, and leaving the forest really amounted to no more than that by daylight.

Ames put a hand to his mount's bit. Then, trying to imagine the exact details of the grim drama which had been played out here, he left the woodland pond to its human and equine dead. After that he completed crossing the remainder of the forest tract ahead and regained the town trail about twenty minutes later. Now he stopped his horse and swung astride it, discovering that it could carry him well enough so long as he didn't ask too much of it, and he let it make its own pace and they arrived back in Brayton while most of the town was at breakfast.

Halting outside his home, Ames tied his horse to the fence and went indoors. Here he changed his garments as quickly as he could and lighted a fire in the kitchen. He was tempted to brew coffee and eat some food before doing anything more, but he reckoned that his horse deserved better than to be left standing around longer than necessary. Leaving the house unlocked on this occasion, he went back to where the creature was standing and led it down the street, putting it in at the livery stables and paying for it to be fed grain and properly curried. After that he walked to the stall where his father's handsome overo was standing and—again knowing this to be a case where his parent's property had become his own—paid the mount's stable fees and dressed it with saddle and bit, leading it out onto the street and finally riding it along to his home. Here he dismounted again and tied it in the same position that his bay stallion had occupied not all that long before.

Now Ames returned to the kitchen, where his fire was burning nicely, and brewed a pot of coffee. He also fried himself a pan of bacon and eggs. The night had left him with less than a real appetite, but he forced the food down all the same—holding to the principle that an active body must be fed—and then he drank a quart of coffee and sat thinking unhappily about what the events of the night had told him.

His beautiful Laury Bergen, the beloved in whom he had been prepared to excuse so much, could no longer be excused. She appeared to be mixed up in something pretty grave. There had been the clear suggestion that she was bringing Joe Fullwood and company information of some kind. Well, working as she did for the Hillwood Stage and Freight Office, she was unquestionably in the position to do that, for she must have reliable access to all kinds of transport information that would be of the utmost worth to a gang of road agents. She could well have been behind any number of stage hold-ups and mining shipment thefts, and that meant criminal guilt of a serious nature. Yet worse still had been the hints that the crooks were holding a woman against her will. This suggested kidnapping, and the penalty for that was life imprisonment. Additionally, and worst of all—as they carried a possible death penalty for those concerned—were the murders of his father and Deputy Sheriff Frank Broom. In fact everything accumulated into an horrendous bill of crime and, should it all be brought home to those responsible, would mean that Laury's life was forfeit with the rest. True, she might dodge the hangman and go to prison for many years; but, however that worked out, she would be finished with love and marriage and Ames must forget her at once in the romantic sense.

Very well. Harrowing as he found it, he would keep this strictly practical. What he needed now, the better to forward his private investigation, was an insight into what his father had known—or suspected—concerning Rex Mills, Laury, and the crooks with whom they were involved. He had earlier supposed a glimpse of this kind to be out of the question, but he had since had new thoughts about that. As the sheriff Hank Ames had been duty bound to keep a log-cum-day book. Some outline of what he had thought and done would undoubtedly be written therein. Presumably the log was lying in his desk at the law office and could be got to without much difficulty.

Ames considered that part of it more closely. When gunned down yesterday, the sheriff had been out patrolling the town, which meant that he would have locked up behind him on leaving the law office as a matter of habit. Probably, with the incumbent's murder throwing everything into chaos, the building was still locked and would stay so until such time as the members of the Peace Committee decided to open it up to their next appointee. Therein lay an opportunity of sorts for Ames, since the locked door should prove no problem to him. He was aware that his father had always kept a second key to the law office at home—against the risk of the regular one getting lost or stolen—and Ames had no doubt that it was to be found up in his late pa's bedroom right now.

Leaving the kitchen table, Ames climbed the stairs and entered the deceased's sleeping place. The dead man's bed was unmade, but everything else in the room was much as his son remembered, and Ames went to his father's war chest—which stood in the rear left-hand corner of the room beside the washstand—and lifted its lid. After a bit of rummaging, he found and unfastened the big leather wallet in which Hank Ames had always kept the smaller of the objects important to him. The key was there. He saw it jammed between a little muslin bag of gold coins and another holding a stickpin and some fancy shirt studs. Removing the key, he thrust it into a trouser-pocket, then closed the wallet again and returned it to the war chest. After that, with all things replaced as he had found them, Ames withdrew from the bedroom and walked back downstairs.

He headed for the front door now, intending to walk straight out into the street; but, pausing abruptly, with his hand upon the door knob, he asked himself whether he had really given enough consideration to precisely what it was he planned to do. Yes, he was a fellow who liked to get things done—and he was never afraid to push matters when he had to—but he had always been careful to ensure that he kept whatever he did strictly legal. What he had in mind here was somewhat less than that. He had no bounden right to use his father's spare key to enter the law office, and being the late sheriff's son hardly provided the moral licence to pry into official business; but, short of entering the grey area in which his needs could be satisfied, he must inevitably condemn himself to more blundering in his movements against the outlaws when his father's desk might give up that little extra knowledge that he required to be exactly sure of what he was facing. He supposed that he was arguably seeking confirmation of what he believed he had already deduced more than anything else—and, even if he came by that, it might not help his future actions all that much—yet the raw details of knowing were often creative in themselves, and it might yet prove that there was more human help to be found in this business than he had thought likely. Anyway, if he should be interrupted in his trespassing and taken to task, he would just have to invent some plausible excuse for his nosing around. While Jim Ames obviously had no right to any special privileges, he *had* been the sheriff's son, and that must account for something.

Now he opened the door and stepped outside. In a few moments he had reached the street and turned eastwards. The stores had opened for the day, and folk were around, a few chatting, but most moving busily and engrossed in their own business. There were also oddments of vehicular traffic on the main. Keeping his eyes averted, Ames entered into the spirit of the hour and called the least attention to himself that he could. So far as he could tell, he reached the law office—which stood in a cutback on the left of the way—without calling a single interested glance to his presence.

If self-effacing in one sense, Ames was

perfectly open as to his presence in the other and stood foursquare as he tried the office door. It was locked, as he had expected, so he took out his key and did what was necessary, pushing the door open after that and leaving the key in the lock. Then he stepped into the gloomy room where his father had held sway for so many years, and went over to the desk, turning in at the back of it and pulling out the big drawer above the knee hole. Now he gazed down upon the neat display of its contents with a probing eye.

He saw the ledger that Hank Ames had used as a log book almost immediately. It lay on top of a sheaf of official-looking papers at the back of the drawer. He lifted it out and, placing it at the middle of the desktop, opened it at the pages which contained his pa's final entries and read what was written there. The last four entries contained the kind of material which he had expected to find, and they claimed his whole attention at once. They went as follows:

September 15th 1882.
A quiet day in town. Mostly routine. Caught up with outstanding office work. Even more worried about Laurel Bergen.

91

September 16th 1882.
News of stage hold-up between Rock Springs and South Pass. A Hillwood coach, Charlie Pearce driving. It could so easily have been that girl again. As despatch clerk, she has access to all the Hillwood way lists. She is seeing Rex Mills regularly, and I have no doubt that he is involved in crooked doings. The man spends money like water, but does no work. I have despatched my deputy, Frank Broom, into the Medicine Bow. He hopes to obtain proof of the connection that we believe exists between Mills and the gang of outlaws who are probably hiding somewhere up there. Otherwise, this has been an average day.

September 17th 1882.
This has been a worrying day. Our biggest rancher, Jeff Frayleson, slipped in to see me early on. His daughter Mary has been kidnapped. Joe Fullwood and his gang are responsible. Frayleson is required to pay a ransom of fifty thousand dollars to get Mary back. Fullwood has warned that Frayleson must not call in the law. The gang will cut Mary's throat if her father does anything but pay up. Frayleson has started reducing assets to put together the ransom money. This will

take a few days, and the crooks are being stalled to that extent. I can do little until Frank Broom gets back. Much depends on what he has to tell me. While I believe Jeff Frayleson has behaved correctly, there can be no doubt that he has taken a fearful risk in coming to the law.

September 18th 1882.

All is well here in Brayton, but this has been one of my most frustrating days as a peace officer. So much seems to be hanging fire. Frank Broom has a free range 'tis true, but I feel he ought to have got back before this. There is still no sign of him. I have had no further word from Frayleson either, though he can't have much to say that he hasn't already said. His problem is one that must be solved. If nothing helpful turns up, I shall have to risk taking a posse into the mountains tomorrow—or the next day at the latest.

That was it. 'Tomorrow' had been the last day of Hank Ames's life, and this was the 'next day'. Every man left a little of something undone at his life's end, but the sheriff had left more than most. Not that he could be blamed for it. The question now was whether his son could save Mary

Frayleson—who was remembered by Jim from earlier years as a dark and lovely girl with gentle manners and a friendly disposition—while attempting to avenge his father's murder. At least he had a clear idea of where to seek the Fullwood gang, which was more than the local law had appeared to have done, and he had no doubt that he would be operating much closer to home than the sheriff and his deputy had imagined. Yet even so, with the little extra that he knew, his situation also had great drawbacks. For whereas Hank Ames could have called on the town for a posse whenever he wished, his son must remain an army of one. While a man alone might achieve much as a scout, he needed others at his back when it came to the fighting, and a battle here might not be too far off. Hardened criminals seldom gave up without a fight, and you couldn't outsmart such men all the time. But things were as they stood, and Ames had to accept them for the moment. Anyway, the loneliness of his position was the greater part of his protection for now.

Just then Ames sensed that he was no longer alone. Looking up sharply, he saw a darkly handsome man, both athletic and well-dressed, standing in the office doorway. The newcomer's brown eyes, bright with intelligence, were fixed on him piercingly, and he felt himself flinch before the other's so far unvoiced accusation. 'Who are you?' came the demand.

'Well, I recognize you anyhow, Mr Frayleson,' Ames said.

'Jim—Jim Ames?'

Ames nodded. 'You haven't seen me in a few years. Not since I grew up.'

'Not since you used to bring the newspapers and mail out to my ranch,' Frayleson agreed. 'I've heard a rumour concerning your father. Is it true?'

'He's dead, yes,' Ames replied. 'It happened yesterday afternoon. He was bushwhacked, here in town, on the main street.'

Letting out a heavy sigh, the rancher shook his head. 'I despair of my fellow man, I really do. Who did it, Jim? Do you know?'

'I know. But I'm not sure I could prove it—as yet.'

'Who?'

Ames shrugged, gnawing at his lower lip in the uncertainty of how much he ought to say. 'All right. I guess we're in this together. I'm after Rex Mills. The shot was fired from high on the Moosegate hotel. Outside Fanny Beales's window. I found the cartridge case there. Springfield-Allin rifle.'

Frayleson grunted sapiently. 'Sounds like you know about my girl.'

'Yes.'

'What are you doing in here, Jim?' the cattleman asked flatly.

'Drawing the threads together.'

'Do you have permission?' Frayleson inquired, glancing pointedly at the scuffed ledger which lay open on the desktop.

'Doubt not.'

'Well, I can understand that you wish to avenge your dad.'

'I want to save your daughter too.'

'Where's your authority, Jim?'

'Why ask? It's obvious I don't have any. What's more, I don't feel the need for any.' Ames saw Frayleson frowning. 'There's too much that needs doing quickly, and folk in authority always want to slow matters up.'

'So what have you to go on?' the cattleman demanded. 'I don't see how you can have a mortal thing. And that's dangerous. It could even be lethal where

96

my girl's concerned.'

'I've been reading what my father wrote about it,' Ames responded. 'I'm not speaking ignorantly.'

'I can't take the risk of letting you rile up a hornets' nest,' Frayleson observed. 'I insist that you back off. We must both look to Frank Broom for justice.'

'The deputy?'

'Your father sent him out on an investigation.'

'I know Broom won't be coming back.'

'What?'

'I found his body up in the pinewoods first thing today,' Ames explained— speaking hesitantly after that, but gradually deciding that the other might as well know all that he knew and drifting into a full and reasonably detailed account of everything which had happened to him since his return to Brayton the day before. 'I don't suppose I know the lot,' he concluded, 'but I reckon I know as much about this as anybody still living.'

'It's a facer about Frank Broom,' Frayleson muttered disconsolately. 'Good man; they don't come much better. But I must admit you seem to know far more than I'd have credited. You think my daughter Mary is actually being held prisoner up there?'

'Damned sure of it,' Ames returned. 'The facts are plain enough, aren't they? You have Joe Fullwood to deal with, and Joe's at home on that ridge up yonder. As I just told you, I heard a woman scream out in the night while I was up there myself. Yes, it's possible it was somebody else. But I don't see who. I'd stake my bottom dollar it was your daughter.'

'You mentioned a cave, didn't you?'

'Among the things I overheard, a cave was spoken of, yes.'

'I don't know of a cave up there.'

'Should you?'

'I know that ridge like the palm of my hand,' the rancher explained irritably. 'This is my country, boy. I've hunted up there dozens of times.'

'Then you should know,' Ames acknowledged. 'Yet there's no mistake on my side either. I heard what I heard.'

Frayleson gestured that they had a kind of impasse, then stepped into the office and moved somewhat heavily over to the desk. 'Just what do you have in mind?'

'First I trust my own judgment,' Ames

replied, feeling that the other had concentrated his mind for him. 'Find that cave, and fetch your daughter out of it.'

'All pretty obvious, I suppose,' Frayleson said. 'Any chance it could prove that easy?'

'Not a hope in hell!'

'I get more afraid of what I've done by the minute,' the rancher admitted. 'If Fullwood gets wind of this—'

'What can you do about what the spirit prompts?' Ames asked rather helplessly. 'I guess I was sort of praying just now for help; and there's nobody could give me more of that than you, by God! But I can see clearly now what I must have simply known before. This *is* a job for one man—at least up to the showdown.'

'I've got two dozen men who'll fight to the death for Mary.'

'You've got two dozen and one,' Ames assured him.

'That had a noble sound to it, Jim,' Frayleson said ironically. 'I'm sure you said it to make me feel better, but I know the power of self. My girl isn't your main concern. It's vengeance you're out for, and I wonder how far you'd let her fate interfere with that. There are clearly other considerations too. You mentioned the Bergen girl, and it's common knowledge how you feel about her. It's likewise known how thick she is with Rex Mills. You must be packing a fair load of worry around, and no man can be single-minded when he's like that.'

'I'm all you've got,' Ames said deliberately—'unless you want to get into the action yourself. You're a smart man, Mr Frayleson, and I may have hampered myself by telling you too much. Sure, I want Mills, but I'm conscious of how important your daughter is in all this. As for Laury Bergen, I've shaken loose—because I must. This awful business is all of a piece when you come to think of it. Serve one, serve all, eh?'

Frayleson nodded reluctantly. 'I suppose that puts it into words about as perfectly as it can be put. There's no law left, so I've got to place trust in you. You are—'

He got no further, for a gunshot cut him off. He staggered forward, planting both hands on the desktop to support himself. 'My goodness!' he breathed.

Ames saw that the rancher was going to fall. He began running round the desk to give support. But the rancher's knees buckled before he could reach the man. Frayleson slipped towards the floor, and came to rest with an ominous thud.

SIX

Ames heard a voice that was low and fearful—almost hysterically anxious indeed —cursing to itself outside the street door, and he became conscious of a lean, slightly stooped figure hovering there, hat pulled forward to obscure the upper face. Jerking his own revolver, Ames perceived that the other, smoking pistol raised and thumb hooking, was having some difficulty to see him properly and shifting about to bring him into clear view. He formed the impression that, though the gunman had a plain enough vision of him to shoot, the fellow wanted to be sure that his next shot was a killing one—which suggested that he could have muddled his targets to start with—and Ames seized on the momentary delay and cuffed off a shot as swiftly as he knew how, the man outside venting an instant cry and staggering backwards, visibly hit high on the body.

Springing forward, Ames made for the street door, and he glimpsed the gunman facing right and starting off down the street at a stumbling run. Bounding outside, Ames saw the broad of his would-be killer's retreating back. He aimed between the other's shoulder-blades, fully intending to cut the fellow down without mercy, but then the fugitive seemed to regain his courage and jerked to a halt, turning about once more. He was revealed now as Claude Vestry—that friend of Rex Mills who had yesterday tripped Ames up while they were drinking together at the time of the sheriff's murder—and Vestry, his angular face shadowed by terror, let out a yell of self-encouragement and began punching shots at the man standing outside the law office door.

Ames shrank from the hail of leaden slugs, but kept his nerve and marked his spot on the figure standing not twenty feet away. He fired, Vestry jerked together, momentarily kicking up his heels and embracing himself; then, legs giving way, collapsed onto his left side. He lay there in the dust at the eastern end of the cutback, impossibly twisted, mouth and eyes wide open, and a scarlet stream running out of his blasted heart and pooling beneath him.

Running up to the fallen man, Ames required but a single glance to know that Vestry had already died. A sort of dismay came over him then. Though forced to it, he had just slain a man, and he believed that another lay dead behind him. These were grim doings, and such incidents had to be explained. Nor would those who required the explanations allow this to be done quickly or without a fuss. A small age would be taken up by the interrogation, and the whole town would be full of his name and what he had done—or was said to have done. There would be talk of murder and such, and rumour would spread all over the auction like ripples about a stone tossed into a pond. He still had this feeling that Vestry—doubtless put up to it by Rex Mills and the enemies that his name had gained amidst the uncertainties of the purblind happenings up on the ridge last night—had been out to kill him with that first shot but had dropped Jeff Frayleson by mistake. The rancher's underhand dealings with the law were most probably still unknown to the Fullwood gang—and could remain so while there was no big outcry here in Brayton and names went unnamed—which meant that he could well remain free to ride both on Mary Frayleson's account and his own if he didn't allow himself to get involved with these doings as yet. Nor was this so implausible, when you came to think of it. At the first sound of shooting, it was sure that everybody on the street would have dived for cover. Thus it was almost equally certain that, at this moment, nobody in town had a clear idea of what had just happened or who had been involved. So, if he ducked out right now, he might well be able to operate with no check on his movements for the rest of the day—and perhaps much longer.

There was an alley on his left. It passed between the end of the law office and the nearest wall of the saddler's shop adjoining. Ames dived into the narrow way. He ran down it and out into the lots beyond. Now he moved to the limit of the sheds and privies there, then turned to his left and hurried back towards his own part of town. He kept his face averted—in case he should meet somebody or was being watched from a bedroom window on his left—but nothing of any kind happened to worry him further, and he regained his home without even hearing an outcry from the direction of the law office. It was all very reassuring.

Yet a man with any sense didn't push his luck too far. So Ames freed his late father's horse from the fence to which he had tied it and mounted up, riding quietly out of town after that with an increasing sense of relief upon him—but also the vague feeling that he was being pushed by circumstances beyond his control and had just been committed to a dangerous task almost against his will. He guessed he was mainly the victim of his own natural reluctance to start anything—and he knew that more venture wilted in the hesitation than the doing—yet he could have done with a short spell of planning and genuine rest before setting out.

This odd sense of deprivation lingered, but he asked himself, as he rode over the trail along which he had shadowed Laurel Bergen through last night's fitful moonlight, what there was to plan. This whole affair had a kind of impromptu touch about it. He had ridden into a situation here that he would have supposed impossible while in Cheyenne. Things just kept happening, events just kept building—little was concrete, less was certain, and he might still climb up yonder, to where the trees ended and the cold airs ran, and discover that he had misread everything and there was nothing to find. He couldn't believe it so, and yet he had no sense of anything definite against which real provision could be made. Too much of this had the formless quality of a bad dream. But perhaps he was just tired. At least the kidnapping of Mary Frayleson and the deaths of men were real enough. Unhappily.

Having made up his mind anew to accept things as they came—because that was how it had to be—Ames approached the area in which he would soon have to leave the trail and climb up through the pine forest in the direction of the ridge for which he was bound. Only too aware that his enemies might keep a daylight watch on this trail—and that he could already be under observation—Ames passed an uneasy eye across the naked ramparts ahead of him and way up to his right, following the wall of stone until it blended with the greater masses north of here and ended in the white peak of the Medicine Bow mountain itself. Well, what he was doing was all about risks, and he was taking a risk, so he had better recognize it and stop feeling gutless. Recalling his thoughts on the path that Laury Bergen must have ascended into the woods last night, in order to visit the Fullwood gang, Ames sought along the right-hand edge of his road for signs of the track, and he came upon them, still waterlogged from the previous night's rain, where grass bearing sunken hoofmarks hollowed into a bed of reeds and then rose through bushes into the first of the pine trees.

Knowing the horse beneath him to be up to it, Ames deliberately jumped the brute over the hollow and onto the slope beyond, scrambling it into the bushes after that and upwards into trees—only removing all goading pressure from its ascent when both were fully hidden by the coarse green foliage and the narrow, root-stepped path which undoubtedly served this end of the ridge was visible before them in the dim light as a presence which could not be mistaken.

Taking his time, Ames travelled warily,

and he reckoned that he was a good many hundred feet up when he was forced to accept a facer, for the well-incised path came to an abrupt end against a variety of granitic outcrops and gave place to a many-fingered tracework that went probing upwards among the jagged rock shapes and into the trees and bushes on either hand. Some of the tracks had obviously been made by game, but others had the stamp of human activity about them, and Ames drew his mount's head round to the right and then urged the creature through a patch of undergrowth that appeared to have been trampled in a similar manner plenty of times before.

Moving northwards now, and soon passing beyond a second lot of granitic outcrops on his left, Ames began drifting upwards again, remembering that he had done much the same in the darkness of the previous night. It wasn't long before he saw the edge of the pinewood above him and made out the ribbed cliffs which went soaring cloud-high into the sunless skies of this day's grey noontide.

Keeping just inside the timber, Ames studied the base of the ridge adjacent through the gnarled boles that covered him, seeking signs of the outlaws' cave, but he spotted nothing whatsoever to encourage him. He persisted with his usual doggedness, and had come to the belief that doing things at hazard required the strongest faith of all—since seekers didn't always find—when, on glancing across a narrow clearing which had appeared directly before him, he saw a rider approaching through the trees on the further side of the space who gave the impression of being no less cautious and even more preoccupied than he.

Ames pulled his horse to the most gentle of halts. Putting his hand upon the butt of his revolver, he sat watching the other, fully conscious that the man had only to lift his head square and fix his eyes for a moment to spot him among the trees on this edge of the clearing. He waited for it, ready to draw and fire when the split second of real need arrived, but the horseman across the way looked up no more than enough to see what he was doing and turned right on entering the clearing. He then shifted in his saddle and prodded his mount into a trot up the hill which the foot of the ridge above must soon check or divert.

Giving the other man plenty of room,

Ames let the fellow reach the top of the climb and come left before shaping in the same direction himself and beginning to shadow the rider up through the trees on what had been his own side of the clearing. Suddenly perceiving that he had allowed himself to drop too far behind, Ames fed his horse the rowels and was soon climbing much faster than his quarry had done. He spotted the other again almost at once, through the boles and fir boughs ahead, as the man crossed the T above him and slipped southwards through the dwarfing shadow of the ridge.

Pushing still harder and breaking back across the angle created by his quarry's lead, Ames neared the limit of his ascent and slowed his mount while a ribbon of cover remained to him, rising in his stirrups to peer over the undergrowth before him and seek the other rider on the ground above the forest edge, but he blinked and felt his heart give a startled jump as he realized that the man—who ought to have been well in sight—had disappeared.

Filling his lungs, Ames vented a whistling gasp. He felt his spine magnetize, and the weirdness of the moment thrilled him strangely. Things like this didn't happen. That man had been real enough, and his horse too. Was it possible that the other had detected the presence of his follower and swung back down into the trees, with a view to coming right round and taking his shadower from the rear? Ames threw an anxious glance over his right shoulder. Nothing there, and the trees grew sparsely at this height, which meant that his still travelling eye—now averted—ought easily to pick out a rider manoeuvring in the shadows down slope of him. More. His ear would have detected such movements too. No, his quarry had simply vanished—and it was up to him to discover how and where.

Risking it, Ames drifted to his right and broke out into the open. He drew rein, then sat and studied the scene directly ahead. There was a certain amount of bush growth along the foot of the ridge in this area. Here and there, the masses of brambles and blackthorn were quite substantial, and a man bent on it could still take cover behind the screening leaf at this season of the year. Ames worked up saliva, quailing before the rifle muzzle that could even now be sighted on his chest;

but nothing stirred, and his horse picked up a hoof and wrinkled its hide, impatient of this unfamiliar rider and wishing to be doing again.

Nudging the brute in close to the prickly growth and the rearing stone behind it, Ames peered closely after any break in the bushes that might have a forced appearance, and all at once his eye lighted on a faint indentation of the wet grass which thinly carpeted a natural gap that led up to a vast slab of rock which lay back against the base of the bluff behind it like the broken pinion of a great bird that had given up hope of life and set itself to die.

Ames dismounted, bending into the gap. He now made out the presence of several dim hoofmarks, but these traces could mean much or nothing. Straightening, he left his horse and entered the break in the bushes, approaching the mass of stone which seemed to not quite belong to the body of the cliff; then, coming to the slab, he followed its length and turned its end, seeing that a considerable opening was concealed behind it—one that would certainly admit a rider and his beast with no trouble at all—and he entered the aperture and found himself at the start of a jagged tunnel that was really a stress fracture which had been caused by a shift in the foundations of the ridge perhaps tens of millions of years ago.

After pausing to give his nose a tentative scratch, Ames moved deeper into the passage, the light soon starting to fade around him, and he dug after a match but found that his pockets were empty due to his earlier hasty change of yesterday's wet clothing. He inched onwards, cursing the lack brought on by his oversight, and reckoned that he would retreat as soon as the darkness about him became complete; but, when this happened, the soft neighing of a horse from somewhere not far ahead drew him onwards, and it was a matter of moments only before he found himself in a vaulted cavern of truly enormous dimensions which was illuminated by rents in the rock wall at its distant back that somehow reminded Ames of a description that he had once read of the great windows behind the high altar in the cathedral of Notre Dame in Paris.

He stood in awe of what he had found, yet was not so badly struck that he did not take in the whole of his surroundings, since there was more here of interest than just the vast cavern itself. On his left, if dimly seen this far from the sources of light, was a bay in which a number of horses were ground-tied and, almost directly ahead of him—beyond big heaps of naturally polished granite balls and at a distance that could not be too great—he could discern an egress which appeared to connect this inner place with a traversable plane, on the same level, in the daylight beyond it.

Ames felt himself instinctively drawn towards this exit and, groping through the broad ribbons of gloom that misted between the light beams of varying intensity that illuminated the cavern, he headed for it—all too aware with every uncertain step that he could be in very grave danger, for the man whom he had seen in the forest had undoubtedly come through here and the horses in the bay behind him warned that a number of other men were not far away. That he was within hailing distance of the Fullwood gang was a virtual certainty, and he could now well appreciate why Jeff Freyleson had been so certain that there was no cave upon this ridge. This mighty rock chamber was indeed wonderfully hidden, and it would surely rate among the great natural finds of the century when its presence was made known generally and visits could be started.

Always testing the floor ahead of him for pitfalls, Ames approached the exit which had recently engaged his attention. The cavemouth was much larger then he had imagined and admitted a lot of light close up. Ames breasted out into the glow of day, blinking a little, and found himself standing at the back of a ledge which curved across the face of a cliff for a distance of about seventy yards and had a maximum reach forward of the egress of twenty yards or more, which made it a large and very safe platform from which to gaze down upon first the green miles of Wyoming's mountain ranges and then the rugged places further west of here.

Suddenly a burst of jeering laughter reached Ames from the right, and he heard men's voices raised in disbelief. He swung towards the sounds, fearing that he was about to be discovered, but saw nobody on the ledge itself. What he did instantly deduce, though, was that Fullwood and company had their hideout in that direction—and, backing up against the cliff wall on that side of the egress, he began side-stepping towards the point from which the noise had originated, only checking when he found himself within a yard of the entrance to what he imagined from the speech echoes must be a large cave.

Feeling very exposed—backed up there against sharp stone and ruffled by the thin, piercing wind which swept across the face of the high rock—Ames was tempted to withdraw at once and reckon himself lucky to still have the chance; but curiosity got the better of his apprehension and he pressed as close to the opening as he dared, ears straining after every syllable that was being spoken within. 'What the tarnation hell's so funny about it, you guys?' he heard a high-pitched male voice bleat aggrievedly. 'The guy's human, ain't he, and a widower too? Stands to reason there's some place he goes to get his socks darned. Anyhow, I'm a-tellin' you: He weren't at that god-damned ranch house of his when I got there this morning, and that's that.' There was a smouldering pause. 'It was your fault, Joe. I'm blamin' you, suh. You should've made a firm arrangement for that man Frayleson to be at home. You've wasted my morning for me, that's what you've done.'

'Will you quit your bellyaching, Simmonds?' demanded a deep voice that Ames recalled from the previous night as Joe Fullwood's. 'Do you figure you're here to catch up on your rest? If so, you think again, my man. This is what we do for a living, and I'm in charge. You do as you're told. Nothing I order you to do is a waste of time. Like hell it is! You were sent to keep Frayleson on his toes. Got that?'

'What's that supposed to alter?' inquired the squeaky but defiant tones of the man named Simmonds. 'Why didn't you tell that cattleman I'd be riding over to his place this morning?'

'I figured he'd have too much on his mind for gallivanting anyhow,' Fullwood grated. 'You expect to count too much with me, Harry. That guy's got plenty on his plate. He's pushed to get that ransom money of ours together. It's no picnic for him.'

'He's probably gone to the bank, Simmonds,' the voice of Rex Mills put in.

'What do you know about it, Mills?'

117

Simmonds asked truculently. 'Are you going to keep littering up this place now you've made town too hot for you?'

'Did all of us a service, didn't I?' Mills asked dangerously. 'Be reasonable, blast you!'

'I don't trust that cowman,' Simmonds said. 'He's slippery. He was told to keep out of Brayton.'

'We don't know he's gone into town,' Fullwood said judiciously. 'That's just Rex surmising. There'd have been no sense in tying down Frayleson—after what we'd demanded. He knows what the penalty will be if he double-crosses us.'

'Aw, you ain't goin' to cut that gal's throat!' Simmonds scoffed. 'Nobody gets paid if you do her in!'

'If Frayleson double-crosses us,' Fullwood reminded, his voice greatly hardened, 'nobody will get paid, full stop. I'll slit her gullet all right, never you fear! But when I make a deal with a guy, I give him every chance. That's my principle.'

'Especially when you can't avoid it, eh, Joe?' Mills chipped in dryly.

'Particularly then,' Fullwood agreed brazenly, laughing at the absurdity of his moral stand. 'Must say, I hope whatever's going on, something more's happening in town this morning than a possible visit by Jeff Frayleson to the bank.'

'Rely on Laury,' Mills responded negligently. 'She'll have spoken to Claude Vestry first thing. My pal will have picked the right time and place. Never was a backshooter like him.'

'That's a hell of a recommendation!' spat a voice that had not been heard before. 'I wouldn't want a pal like that!'

'Nor would I, Milligan,' Fullwood commented. 'But the varmint clearly has his uses.'

'With a name like Claude he'd need to!' the unseen Milligan tittered. 'You ever hear the like?'

'Plenty of times,' Fullwood answered. 'Clarence and Archibald too. Some women'd name their sons God Almighty.' He spat audibly. 'Hey, Fenner! How's the grub coming along?'

'All in the pot, Joe,' another voice which had been silent until now drawled in answer. 'Salt's what we need. Anybody got a pinch o'salt?'

'You're salty enough for ten!' Fullwood scoffed.

'Ain't that right, boss?' Fenner agreed

119

cheerfully. 'And there ain't but seven of us. Eight if you count the girl. But her mouth's stuffed full of gag!'

'We have to take care of her figure for her,' Fullwood observed caustically. 'Nothing like keeping a woman's trap shut for that. A little starve will do that noisy wench a heap of good!'

There was further haw-hawing, and the listening Ames reckoned that he had overheard enough. His problem now was how best to handle what needed doing here. There were too many of the outlaws to tackle alone. A fellow couldn't safely hold more than two or three desperate men at gunpoint in a complex situation. More than that, day or night, and he soon needed eyes in the back of his head. If only he could go back to town and ask for assistance, but he knew that he couldn't risk that. Even if his story of what was going on up here were fully credited, the chances were that any suspicions concerning him would cancel out his plea for help. No, he'd have to do the only thing that was really left to him—ride around the southern end of the ridge and then across the grass opposite him now and onto Jeff Frayleson's Circle F. He ought to be able to get all the help that he needed there—though, in the circumstances he feared it likely that the staff of the Circle F didn't know that the daughter of the ranch had been kidnapped. Well, he would have to sort all that out with the people involved when the time came. The thing now was to make a quick retreat from here and get to the Frayleson ranch house with the least possible delay.

Side-stepping to his left, Ames began moving away from the edge of the cavemouth. It all seemed so childishly simple, and he thanked heaven that the badmen—no doubt regarding themselves as perfectly concealed—had posted no look-out on either side of the ridge. Hurrying his actions when he considered it safe to do so, he made to turn through the entrance to the great cavern at the heart of the ridge, but had barely started the movement when the muzzle of a rifle jammed hard beneath his ribs and he realized that he must after all have got things wrong somewhere. 'Back the way you came, Jim!' a female voice ordered tautly.

'Laury?' Ames yelped, glimpsing the auburn-haired beauty from the tail of his eye.

'Do what I say!' she ordered, prodding hard.

He obeyed. It was clear that his love no longer had any affection for him whatsoever.

SEVEN

This was a real emergency. Ames summoned up the whole of his will. When it had come to a mental battle in the past, he had usually been able to overcome Laurel Bergen's mind, and it had to be worth a maximum effort to gain the ascendancy over her now. What she did not know—or at least could not be certain about—was that he had overheard what had passed between her and Rex Mills in the dark of the woods last night and knew her fear of death on the gallows. Now he decided to use his knowledge in the most destructive manner he could and, picking his words with the most calculated brutality, looked her in the eyes and said: 'Hold hard there, Laury. I get visions these days, and I just had one. I saw a hard-featured man taking you off the gallows rope. Your neck was broken like that of a Christmas goose, and your tongue was bitten clean through. Beside you stood a plain deal coffin, and another man was getting ready to put you—'

'Shut up!' the girl breathed hoarsely, ashen-faced and shuddering from head to toe. 'I'll shoot you if you don't!'

'Can't you face the truth?' he asked.

'Truth!' she quivered. 'Jim, you—'

'Sweetheart,' he interrupted, switching to his softest and most sincere, 'it's going to turn out just as I pictured if you don't stop it this moment. I reckon I can still save your life if you take that gun off me and go home. That's what you have to do. Go home—and stay there! Let me work out what's here to work out. Just along the cliff from here is the worst of bad company. I'm as sure as eggs that lot's going to swing before all's done. If you go on with them now, you'll hang too—and it won't be long before it happens.'

The girl appeared to weaken, and her chin began to droop; but then her delicate mouth hardened and her stare became coldly feline. 'I know what you're doing,' she accused. 'You were always doing it to me. That's how you talked me into being your girl. You made me feel I needed looking after.'

'And don't you?' Ames asked.

'You think you know what's best for people,' Laury said hotly, the colour rushing back into her pallid cheeks. 'You're just like your old father, and your mother wasn't much better. You Ameses only know what's best for you. I soon found how different it was with Rex Mills. He treats me like a woman, lets me do what I want, and never tries to take over. It was plain wicked how you talked me into things before you went off to Cheyenne and—and left me here to—to await your future wishes. I was gulled, Jim, that's what I was, and I'll never let myself be talked into anything like that again. You hear me?'

'You're making it all up!' Ames protested.

'No, I'm not!'

'Then you're twisting it all!' he moderated. 'When folk go by twos, one or t'other has to plan their path. Otherwise they go walking off as they like and get lost.'

'As they like!' Laury Bergen insisted, the beating of her heart so violent that it was

124

visible through the lace front of her blouse. 'As they like! They do what pleases them. Don't you understand? I want what I do to please me. It pleases me to go my own way. That's what I like!'

'Your own way—to the gallows?'

'You bastard!'

'I didn't imagine my honey-tongued Laury knew that word,' Ames said drearily.

'Rex whispers some much worse ones to me at times,' she taunted. 'I'll bet you can guess what they are. You're no saint! You just want everybody else to believe you are. Hypocrite!'

'Maybe,' he conceded. 'You've heard *me*, Laury. Will you go home? Give us both a chance, eh? And if you think I'm treating you rough, I'll tell you this. I know Rex Mills shot my father and I'm certain that you knew it was coming. That makes you an accessory before the fact. But I'm willing to ignore all that, now, indeed everything—if you'll only go home!'

'No, Jim!' she stamped. 'Rex and Joe will kill you, and you'll be out of my life forever!'

'This really is your last chance,' Ames pleaded, certain of it deep in his being. 'What you've been doing at Hillwood Stage and Freight is already strongly suspected. If you lie low—'

'Fiddlesticks!' she cut in disdainfully, letting him feel the dig of her rifle again as she once more urged him to start back along the ledge. 'The gang and I are far too clever for those fools in the office!'

He braced himself anew. If this couldn't be achieved one way, it must be at least attempted another; so he grabbed the barrel of the girl's Winchester and tried to snatch the weapon away from her; but she started back, clutching tight, and the gun went off in the process, its bullet lancing across Ames's lower ribs on the left-hand side and the muzzle-flash burning his shirt. Blood welled up thereafter, and Ames stood looking down at himself. 'Nicely,' he said stonily.

'It was your own fault!' the girl snapped, clearly shocked.

'Too late, Laury,' he said resignedly, hearing loud shouts from the cave of the outlaws and then feet running towards the girl and himself.

Eyes like agates, and features lean and feral, matching the slender erectness of his more than six-foot frame, the man that Ames knew from the past as Rex Mills appeared first from the hideout along the cliff. Behind him came an older man, heavier and squarer, blocky of jaw, walrus moustached, greying at the temples, and carrying a faint air of authority which, at Ames's immediate guess, made him Joe Fullwood. This was at once confirmed when Laury said: 'I caught him out here, Joe. He must have been listening.'

'Jimmy Ames,' Mills said, his voice filled with an angry hiss of contempt. 'You were supposed to have been taken care of elsewhere.'

'It all went wrong, Rex,' the girl informed him.

'Yeah,' Mills agreed distastefully. 'What are you doing here at this hour, Laurel?'

'I'm here *because* it went wrong,' the girl stressed.

'That's plain enough, Mills,' Fullwood said, throwing a hard glance over his shoulder at the knot of unkempt and shabbily clad men pressing up behind him. 'Get back into the cave, you guys!' He pressed a fingertip to his left hairy nostril and blew out mucus through the no less hairy right, at the same time nodding his approval as Mills plucked Ames's sixgun from its holster and thrust the weapon

127

into his own waistband. 'G'damn snout! Bring that polecat along, Laury. It looks to me like he must have latched on behind Harry Simmonds and followed the varmint in here. I sent the wrong man to the Frayleson place all right. I ought to kick his butt!'

'Varmint yourself!' snorted a seedy, perceptibly wall-eyed man, who was otherwise nondescript of face—though vaguely recognizable to Ames as the horseman whom he had indeed followed up here out of the pinewood—from the centre of the bunched outlaws who were now walking back to the cave.

'I *will* kick your butt if you give me much of that!' Fullwood declared. 'And keep in close to the cliff—all of you, blast your eyes! We can do without flitting about up here like fleas. If we ain't careful, my buckos, there'll come a day when somebody down on the grass yonder spots movement up here. And that will be the end of the best hideout north of the Hole-in-the-Wall!'

Ames walked stolidly with the outlaw band. He could feel Laury Bergen's rifle in his back and the blood trickling down his left side. He knew that he wasn't hurt in any degree that mattered, and simply ignored the stinging of his torn flesh, not even pressing a hand to the wound as he turned into the large but ill-formed and smoke blackened cave where the badmen had clearly lived their crude existence for some time amidst their packing case seats, filthy bedrolls, scattered newspapers, and the general bric-a-brac of outlawry.

At the middle of the cave floor, orange and grey within its circle of stones, a woodfire burned—a pot of stew or the like upon its top—and behind it, bound and gagged, a shapely young woman lay. She was clad in a riding skirt, check shirt and leather jacket, and was staring glumly out into the day, her eyes red-rimmed and flakes of ash lying amidst the glossy tresses of her black hair. Ames recognized her instantly as Mary Frayleson, Jeff's daughter, though he hadn't seen the girl in a few years and, regardless of his own hurt and predicament alike, was rather startled to see how perfectly she had matured and how totally her innocent beauty put that of the spoiled Laury to shame.

'Going to hobble Ames?' Mills asked of Fullwood, as the badmen broke up and went to their various places around the cave, either sitting down at once or lounging against the walls.

'I don't know what I'm going to do with him yet,' Fullwood explained.

'Except to kill him?' Mills prompted significantly.

'That's for sure,' the gang-boss agreed, glancing at the pot of grub on the fire. 'But there's no hurry. I do my best killing on a full stomach.'

'He's dangerous as can be, Joe,' Laury Bergen warned.

'The fact he's up here is proof of that,' Fullwood acknowledged, squatting now on a box and fishing the 'makings' out of the breast-pocket of his shirt. 'So what went wrong in town, Laury?'

'He must have been what went wrong,' the girl answered, nodding at Ames—who now stood on her right and opposite the gang-boss—though still under the threat of her Winchester. 'I'm not sure of exactly what took place. Nobody seemed to know that, and I couldn't form a clear picture, but Claude Vestry is dead and Jeff Frayleson has been badly wounded. He's unconscious—so I heard—and Doctor Rutherford can't say whether he'll live or die.'

Fullwood swore sulphurously, spoiling the cigarette that he was rolling and throwing both the tobacco and the paper into the fire. 'If that ain't the—! Where did this happen?'

Laury Bergen glanced down uneasily at Mary Frayleson. 'In the sheriff's office—they say.'

'The sheriff's—!' Fullwood half exploded. 'Aren't you sure about anything, girl?'

'I'm doing my best, Joe,' Laury Bergen pouted.

'You should have stayed in Brayton,' the gang-boss informed her angrily. 'Mights and maybes are of no use to us. What we need—always—is accurate information. If you'd stuck in town, you'd have got the full story before the day's end. Why the haste to get up here? How'd you obtain permission to get away from your work place?'

'I up and went.'

'You did what?' Fullwood roared. 'Couldn't that cost you your job?'

'It may well,' the girl admitted dismally.

'I ought to smack your bottom for that!' the gang-boss declared. 'You're no use to us without that job.'

'Why the haste?' Rex Mills reminded.

'The town is going to send out a posse,' Laury explained.

'Looking for him?' Fullwood asked uncertainly, jerking a thumb at Ames.

'Yes, Joe,' the girl answered. 'Somebody said they'd seen Jim Ames unlock the law office; and somebody else said they saw him leaving town on the west trail.'

'So?' the gang-boss inquired, his face betraying that there was much he didn't yet understand and as to which Laury had better fully satisfy him.

'I couldn't be sure how much Jim knew about us,' the girl further explained. 'I'm not sure now. He was the sheriff's son, and—and if he had been talking to Frayleson—'

'I think you mean if Frayleson had been talking to him.'

'I guess so,' Laury admitted. 'I thought I was doing right, Joe. I did catch Jim for you.'

'Well, Frayleson knows nothing which concerns this hideout,' the gang-boss said, 'so we don't have to worry about that part of it. This seems like a capital foul-up to me, and I'm not certain how best to handle it. The threat could be great or small. What do you think, Rex?'

'I think we should find out what Ames knows,' Mills replied. 'If him and Frayleson met, there must have been talk. What matters to us is what Frayleson might have said.'

Fullwood began a slow and judicious nodding. 'It doesn't follow that he said a word about the abduction of his daughter. If he did, it only really matters if it was passed on, and I don't see how this fellow Ames could have had time to do that.'

'Jim,' Rex Mills said, 'it looks to me like you've got one or two questions to answer. Now, I'm going to personally bust you up if you don't play Honest Injun. But why pile on the agony, mister? You're caught, and you're never going anywhere else. Whatever you know can only be told to us now. You have no life beyond today.'

Ames could see that what the man said was true within the present circumstances and, to avoid getting beaten up, he was prepared to co-operate truthfully in so far as he didn't further jeopardize Mary Frayleson's life. In fact he didn't believe that speaking frankly almost throughout —and including last night—could do much harm. There was the possible bonus too, that if he confirmed most of what these rogues suspected, they would believe the lie that really mattered when it came along. 'Okay, Mills,' he said evenly, 'I've got your message. You ask, and I'll answer.'

'Don't feel tempted to faze us with any smart lies,' Fullwood hurried in. 'I'll be watching you, and I'll know by the signs if we're being deceived. Mary Frayleson's life could be at stake.'

'Don't be too anxious to cut the girl's throat, Joe,' Mills said bluntly. 'It was a good bargaining ploy, but it only comes when we're certain there's to be no pay day.'

'My sentiments exactly,' Fullwood responded. 'The sense of this business is fifty thousand dollars. Take that away and there's no sense.'

'What is all this talk about?' Ames asked contemptuously. 'You'll kill her anyway if her father dies. There's no sense in that either. Why don't you just let her go?'

'The dead give no testimony,' Mills reminded grimly, 'and kidnapping is the next most serious crime to murder.'

'Which is to say,' Ames observed logically, 'you'll end up murdering both her and her father—even if you do somehow come by the ransom money.'

Mills let fly with a terrific backhander. Ames reeled away from the stinging blow, straightening into an even harder one from the opposite direction. He tasted blood and spat, then said: 'I had this figured too. I get the stuffing beaten out of me whatever I say or do. You were always like that, Mills. It's the way of a crazy man—or a killer beast!'

This time Mills let loose with his fist. The blow, a kind of uppercut, buried itself low in the prisoner's abdomen. Turning cold all over, Ames fell to his knees, and had the sense to stay there.

'What is this?' Joe Fullwood demanded. 'Questions, man, questions!'

'Just softening him up!' Mills returned, as if surprised that such a small expedient should have called forth comment; and he seized Ames by the wings of his collar and lifted powerfully, setting the hurt prisoner back on his feet.

More in fear than anger—since he sensed that another blow would not be long in coming—Ames shoved Mills off balance with his right hand and then triggered a left hook, his best punch, and Mills fell as if the legs had been chopped from beneath him. In the same instant, something called Ames's attention to the girl lying behind the fire. He saw both desperate fury and intent in Mary Frayleson's stare. Then, spinning on her posterior, she struck from left to right with raised legs, her booted feet making heavy contact with the cooking pot standing on top of the fire and splashing its contents all over the place—not least among the brands burning beneath it—and there was a puffing, sizzling roar, and clouds of damp ash erupted into the atmosphere, obscuring movement generally.

Ames heard Laurel Bergen spitting and spluttering to his left. Knowing that he had been given his chance, he rounded on the girl and snatched the rifle from her grasp, charging her violently aside as he backed up with the cocked Winchester ported before him. The flying girl cannoned into the seated Joe Fullwood—who had grasped the import of what was happening and already whipped out his gun—and the gang-boss went toppling with her, thus eliminating the most immediate of the threats to the would-be escaper's break for freedom—though the cross-eyed Harry Simmonds got in a shot within the second.

Ames saw the slug whip cloth off the left side of his waistband. He blasted an answer through the drifting haze, and a scream suggested that his bullet had pierced the midriff at which it had been directed. More guns spoke now, reminding Ames that there were four other gunmen present who had yet to be fully introduced. He pumped his rifle's magazine as fast as he knew how and blazed at the gunflashes about him. Again his trousers were touched by a bullet, and other lead sang close. Some of it struck rock and ricocheted waspishly, but most found its way outside and flew harmlessly into the distance.

Realizing that he had no hope of winning a sustained gunbattle against the present odds, Ames shrank low and retreated in earnest. Regaining the ledge, he triggered off three shots in a row, discouraging immediate pursuit. After that he sprang to his right and broke into a run. Going his fastest, he made for the entrance to the great cavern in the rock nearby. Now he heard shouts and the sound of running feet in his wake as the inevitable pursuit began. The ingress appeared on his left. Fetching round sharply, he skidded through it and, pushing himself to the absolute limit still, plunged onwards, reckless of limb and welcoming as a friend the first of the inner areas of almost complete darkness that immersed him.

There was a wildness in Ames. One hundred percent alive, he knew there were obstacles about the floor which could bring him down and injure him seriously. But he dared disaster. His flight through this echoing place was live or die, and he might as well be smashed by his own will as shot down tamely by the gun of a man with greater nerve but probably shorter legs. On, dammit—on! There were horses in that bay at the other side of this place. He'd grab one the instant he reached the spot where they stood—if he got that far—since it was likely that his own horse, left standing by him near the bushes at the other side of the ridge, had been brought indoors by Laury Bergen when she had arrived outside the hideout with fear of the projected posse from Brayton uppermost in her mind.

Light misted upon Ames through one of the natural apertures in the mighty wall now a fair distance to his rear. Suddenly the voice of an outlaw calling to his comrades warned that Fullwood's band had entered the cavern and were boring ahead. Doubtless he, Ames, had just been glimpsed where a tail of daylight rifted—and was a trackable target—but he felt reasonably sure that there would be no indiscriminate firing in here, for the crooks knew as well as he that the force of the reverberations under the roof would be enormous and who could say what the degree of stability was up there? Only fools or lunatics would risk bringing down untold tons of rock upon themselves on the vague chance of hitting an escaper whom they must be fairly confident they were about to recapture anyway.

Ames shut his mind to everything else and just kept going. Then, as if by a miracle—though he barely proclaimed it inwardly—he found himself at the further side of the cavern. It occurred to him then that a man might do about once in a hundred times what he had just done and traverse this darksome hole without a single trip or collision, which meant that he had won out so far at odds of a hundred to one. He heard a snorting, harness jingling softly, and the rasping of a horseshoe on stone. The mounts were directly ahead of him. Yes, he saw a slight movement there.

Then he put his hands on a horse—still holding his rifle in the right as best he could—dragged it away from its ground-tie, and ran it into the faintly discernible neck of the exit tunnel on his left, setting himself to spring upon the brute's back, flatten himself against its mane, and then head for the daylight, mainly relying upon the creature's instinct to get them there.

Now he checked abruptly. This was panic; he was simply reacting to his own fear. There was a girl back there who desperately needed his help. She had created his chance to escape, and he must not ride off and leave her. If he did that, he might never manage to get anywhere near her again. It was imperative that he gather up his courage and make a supreme effort on her behalf right now. He still possessed a gun—and wits enough to recognize the unexpected. Perhaps he could trick these hellions out there. They were keyed to expect his continued flight, and it went without saying that they couldn't see anything of him down here. If he sent the horse clattering off along the tunnel, he believed Fullwood and company would automatically assume that he was still with it. But, with the brute in motion, there would be nothing to stop him from dodging back to his right, crossing the rear of the bay in which the horses stood, and then moving on to some hiding place in the recesses of the cavern. If the outlaws left as a whole body, he would be able to come out of hiding, backtrack to the cave along the ledge, free the girl, and escape with her before Fullwood and company got the first inkling of what he had done.

He must try it. In good conscience, he could do no less.

EIGHT

Raising his left hand, Ames brought its palm down with all his force on the rump of the horse before him. The brute neighed angrily and snapped its teeth at him, then plunged off into the darkness of the tunnel beyond, the clatter of its hooves instantly receding towards the light that it must know to be there. Doubled almost to the floor—in order to avoid any hovering gleam from above—Ames crabbed away to his right and crossed the back of the bay which the remaining horses occupied, raising onto tiptoe then and flitting off into the gloom beyond.

Listening at the largely invisible floor of the cavern—down a line which ended at the further exit—Ames picked up sounds which made him realize that the badmen had been covering ground much faster than he had thought likely and were already quite close. Now rubble shifted under his soles, rattling audibly, and he judged that his continued presence in the cave would be detected by an outlaw ear if he tried drifting still further into the body of the place, so he halted where he was and, discovering with an outstretched hand that a wall was located nearby, pressed his back to the rock and stood motionless, his breathing heavily muted as he traced the last few yards of the badmen's approach to his end of the cave and their entry into the bay where their horses were secured.

There was much jostling and swearing as the men, bent on haste, bumped and collided in the darksome shadows. A match flared, the flame wavering in a disembodied hand, and then a greater light which Ames had not expected came swelling towards him, the outer arc of its glow providing visibility on a curve not so many feet from where the fugitive was standing. Indeed, Ames could have been spotted had the outlaws had any reason to peer into the gloom after him; but, as it was, he was the one who took advantage of a hazy view and watched the badmen backing out their horses from the indent, a process which was only disturbed when Joe Fullwood called: 'One of you must stay behind and keep an eye on the Frayleson girl. Tommy, it had better be you!'

'What's up?' a round-bodied, ageing man asked aggrievedly, his fat, sagging face fully visible to the watcher for a moment as it swung towards his boss.

'Cut it out, Decallow!' Fullwood snarled. 'Are you the youngest and most spry of us? You blamed well know you ain't! It's tricky, riding down there in the forest, and you're no hand at it. Let's hear no more of it now!'

'But what if I get left here permanent?' Decallow complained.

'You won't!' Fullwood retorted, hands on either side of his mount's head as he drew the creature out of the bay and into the tunnel adjacent. Now he bumped shoulders with a similarly backing Mills.

'Blast you, Rex—get on then!'

Movement, rapid and hectic, persisted in the area for several moments longer, but the outlaws sorted themselves out with what was really considerable skill and were soon running their horses down the exit passage and beyond the watcher's ken. Presently only the fat Decallow was left, and he stood scratching his belly and grumbling evilly. Then, picking up the lantern from the raised slab of flat rock on which it was apparently kept, his footfalls moving cautiously out into the body of the cavern after that as he made for the distant outlet which served the western ledge and the gang's hideout itself.

Ames held still against the wall. He knew that he must not begin pursuing Decallow too soon. If something should go wrong, and a fight in the dark result, he could as easily wind up the loser as the winner. Discipline was the keyword. He must keep calm and carefully judge the amount of time needed for each thing he did. A little patience should ensure that he would be able to creep up on Decallow and either take the old guy prisoner or put him out of action at the most propitious moment.

All at once he heard equine noises

from his right. Then he abruptly recalled having seen two horses left in the bay nearby. He suspected that the brutes belonged to Laurel Bergen—who was clearly still around and also had to be reckoned with—and Mary Frayleson, whose garments suggested that she had been kidnapped while out riding. This seemed to mean that his own horse was still standing at the foot of the ridge outside. Well, Laury had appeared to be in a bit of a panic when she had got here, so it wasn't particularly remarkable that she hadn't brought the animal inside after all.

Now Ames saw Tommy Decallow's squat figure outlined against the light that entered through the western egress. Next moment the man's shape disappeared on the right and the glow in the outlet was again untrammelled. Stirring, Ames set off after the ageing badman, pumping at his Winchester as he went and hearing the shell that he had last fired ring softly on the floor as it was ejected beside him. Then, hopefully prepared for all eventualities, he felt his way ahead a little faster and soon reached the exit himself, passing outside into the daylight again and turning in the direction of the outlaws' cave.

Moving in close to the rockface once more, Ames made for the entrance to the hideout with maximum stealth, praying that he wouldn't have to fire his rifle—since it had just occurred to him that the sound of a shot would certainly carry over the ridge and probably bring the Fullwood gang back from their wild goose chase before they were even aware it was such—and it seemed to him that the devil had set his foot when, as he came within a pace of the cavemouth, Tommy Decallow stepped out of it and turned at once to face the catfooting intruder, the ash-coated cooking pot in his hands and held before his breastbone.

The outlaw recoiled slightly, as if he couldn't believe his eyes, then dropped the cooking pot and went for his Colt at a remarkable speed for a man of his age. Acting instinctively—and never for a moment expecting to achieve the result which in fact he did—Ames lunged at Decallow with the muzzle of his Winchester and struck the crook very solidly above the bridge of his nose. Decallow staggered, cumbrous on his stocky legs, and fell backwards, landing on his buttocks and looking a trifle dazed.

Ames prepared to put the muzzle of his rifle to Decallow's forehead again—if much less violently this time—and advise the older man to give up, but the crook still had a grip on his pistol and the expression in his murky eyes warned that he meant to use it at any cost, so Ames struck sideways with his rifle barrel now and knocked his man senseless with the single blow. Decallow folded up into an untidy little heap, and Ames bent and picked up the revolver which had just fallen from the other's limp fingers, thrusting it into his empty holster. After that Ames bounded ahead, spinning to face the interior of the cave, where he saw that Laury Bergen had just run to where Harry Simmonds—whom he had shot earlier—was lying apparently dead. The girl showed every sign of picking up the downed outlaw's pistol and using it offensively against the returned Ames, who now jumped at her with the sole of his left boot raised and shoved her away from Simmonds' inert form. 'Stop it, Laury!' he warned. 'I'll knock you cold too, if I have to!'

'Some lover!' the auburn-haired Laury sneered up at him from the floor on which she was now sprawling. 'It couldn't have gone very deep, could it?'

'You little idiot!' Ames seethed. 'Don't try any of that on me! I gave you your chance, and you threw it back in my face. I'm going to take you home and see you locked in the Brayton cells. That's it, Laury!'

The girl started to weep.

Features remaining stony, Ames shook his head implacably. 'Get up, Laury!' he ordered, glancing quickly at the still bound and supine Mary Frayleson. 'Untie Miss Frayleson!'

Laury hesitated, obviously still calculating behind her tears.

'I mean this instant!' Ames cracked out, essaying a distinctly threatening movement towards her.

Briefly hurrying, Laury Bergen went to Mary Frayleson's side and knelt there.

'Get on with it!' Ames barked. 'And don't pretend your fingers are lily stems; they're strong enough!'

Laury began to pull and tug at the knots, making little impression on them at first; but, after breaking a fingernail or two—and weeping a good deal more as Ames forced her to a real effort—she managed to loosen the bonds, and before long Mary Frayleson was lying free.

Sitting up stiffly, the dark girl removed the gag from her mouth and spat distastefully. 'I didn't expect to see you back here,' she gasped at Ames.

'I had to come,' he responded. 'If I'd left the ridge, there might have been no way back later. With you running free, your kidnappers will have lost their purchase, and we—or others—will be able to move against them as necessary.'

'I suppose so,' Mary Frayleson said uncertainly, clambering shakily to her feet and first easing then massaging limbs which were visibly knotting.

'Bad cramp?' Ames asked a little anxiously. 'How long have you been trussed up like that?'

'Since last night,' the dark girl answered. 'They didn't tie me up to begin with, but I tried to escape. It was after that they got rough and bound me hand and foot.'

Ames nodded, remembering the scream that he had heard from up here while down in the forest the previous night. 'But you are all right?'

'Yes, I'm okay.'

Keeping a watchful eye on Laury Bergen,

Ames walked deeper into the cave, picked up Harry Simmonds' revolver from where it still lay—weighed the weapon while stirring its now clearly defunct owner with a toe—then looked significantly at Mary Frayleson, who promptly stretched out a hand. He passed the weapon to her, frowning; for, if battle were anywhere joined, an armed female was going to get shot at as surely as an armed male, but the rancher's daughter would have the right to defend herself if the need arose, and that seemed to him the lesser of the two evils. After that Ames cast a keen eye about him, seeking other weapons that the gang might have left behind, but there was nothing else visible; and, satisfied that he had drawn the cave's sting in so far as he could, he said: 'Let's get out of here. There are two mounts standing in the cavern yonder, Miss Frayleson. I'd like you to take charge of them, when we get there, and lead them outside.'

'Right,' the dark girl said in a business-like voice, as they walked out of the cave, Ames with a firmly restraining hand on Laury Bergen's left shoulder.

They passed along the ledge, then entered the great cavern adjoining. Familiar with the dimly lighted and echoing rock chamber now, Ames no longer feared any pitfalls, and they walked quite freely down the length of the place and soon came to the rocky bay in which the gangsters had kept their horses. Here Mary Frayleson collected the two mounts still standing there, then moved into the exit passage on the left with Ames and Laury Bergen bringing up the rear. Indeed, it all went so easily that Ames, who had felt the constant need of late to throw the whole of his will behind every action, could hardly grasp that all had been done in a simple and relaxed fashion without the need for any huffing and puffing from him; and he felt quite strange about it when they emerged in the bushes at the eastern side of the ridge and he saw the horse which he had left at this spot an hour or two ago cropping placidly as it waited, apparently untouched by any of the potentially hostile hands which had come this way in the meantime.

After peering around to make sure that they were entirely alone, Ames looked on while Mary Frayleson patted what was plainly her own horse, recovered from the hiding place within, and he stood by when she swung up a few moments later.

Then he gestured for Laury Bergen to do the same, and walked to his overo next, preparing to step astride likewise, but in that moment Laury slapped at her mount and sent the brute plunging towards the treeline directly below them.

Still unmounted, Ames threw his rifle to his shoulder and, steadying the Winchester's barrel across his saddle, aimed at the escaping girl's back. It would have been easy to kill her, but he couldn't bring himself to press the trigger. His emotions were inevitably mixed, though affection was the least of them just then, and it was his moral certainty that to fire the rifle would be tantamount to murder that held him in check. Yes, he perceived the risk that he was taking. Laury might well find her outlaw friends very quickly—and tell them in two dozen words that he had freed their prisoner—but that was still no overpowering reason to shoot her. So he let her go, as he felt sure that she had known he would when she had initiated her apparently suicidal break for it, and he told himself that he and his dark companion had a good start on whatever the future held and that that should be enough.

'Ought I to say anything?' Mary Frayleson asked ironically.

'Better not,' Ames advised, lowering his Winchester's hammer on the cartridge in its barrel. 'I expect you'd heard about Laury and me. Everybody has. Folk don't gossip—much!'

'I'm glad you didn't fire,' the cattleman's daughter said, her upper body twisted towards him as he mounted up. 'It would have been a deed of shame.'

'That miss is one hell of a bad lot all the same,' Ames said grimly.

'You don't have to tell me,' Mary Frayleson reminded. 'I was there during one or two of her visits to that cave, and heard much.'

Ames nodded curtly, his eyes questioning ahead of his tongue. 'Your ranch?'

'It's the only place, isn't it?' she said tightly. 'If we can get there!'

'Off to your right,' he said. 'Let's follow the top of the forest southwards.'

They set off at the gallop, but their path was too steep and narrow—not to mention too pitted and littered with rocks—to let them make haste for long, and they soon found themselves riding at little more than a slow trot which frequently zig zagged.

This was frustrating, especially as their raised line of travel kept them continuously visible to any eyes that might be watching in the trees below, but they were already far south on the ridge and soon arrived at the granitic outcrops which had blocked Ames's earlier ascent and compelled him to turn north across the slope. These same obstructions—which Ames now perceived to sprawl upwards and join to the base of the ridge itself—now forced him to lead his companion down into the trees, where they came presently upon the path that descended to the town trail.

Although unfamiliar with this part of the high terrain, Ames toyed with the ideas of trying to round the outcrops on their underside and then gambling on finding a way to the southern end of the ridge and turning it at much the same elevation as they had been travelling previously; for he imagined that this, if it worked out anything like he expected, would give them the advantage of being able to ride straight down the reverse slope of the formation and reach the western grass with minimum effort and loss of time; but, inviting as all this seemed, he could not ignore the possibility that he and the dark girl would find themselves totally impeded by the stone masses at some stage and be forced to backtrack, perhaps into the path of pursuers who had already glimpsed them; so, after calling a few words of explanation to Mary Frayleson, he turned down the forest track and headed for the trail below, knowing that that, for all the extra effort involved, would take them round the end of the ridge with certainty and also give them sure access to the grass beyond.

The descent was easy enough, even in the nature of a rest for the horses and, when they reached the bottom of the track, Ames stirred up his horse and launched out, showing the girl what he required as he jumped the marshy hollow between the lower treeline and the town trail. Landing perfectly, he rode a dozen yards westwards—in order to leave adequate manoeuvring room at his back—then drew rein, waiting for the rancher's daughter to complete the jump and catch up with him, This she did without mishap, and he was just beginning to feel that they were getting away with it very nicely, when he heard a yell from down trail of them. Turning his head and peering eastwards, he saw the very sight that he least wished to see, for

Fullwood and company were sitting their horses a few hundred yards away and looking towards the girl and himself. His mind speeding, Ames noted instantly that Laury Bergen was not with the outlaws, and he perceived that, as a matter of sheer bad luck, in trying to do his best for Mary Frayleson and himself, he had led them right into the path of their enemies, who had clearly been no more certain of what to do next than he had himself a few minutes ago. Well, it was no good getting depressed about the error; their only course now must be to try outrunning the gangsters. That should be quite possible—since both the girl and he were excellently mounted—but there was no denying that bullets travelled much faster than horses, and he realized that there would be plenty of slugs flying before long.

He said nothing to his companion, but spurred on with a will, and the powerful overo—used to him now—went galloping westwards like a racehorse, drawing Mary Frayleson's black mare after it by the sheer power of its example. They hammered up the trail, little in it for speed, and the trees and rock on their right seemed to change character as their perspective changed. Ames threw a glance across his shoulder. The outlaws had commenced giving chase and were coming on fast. He glimpsed puffs of smoke around more than one outstretched fist, and heard the detonation of the shots a split second later. The bullets missed—or perhaps even fell short—and he turned his face to the front again and pulled his head down, using his spurs relentlessly for the moment.

The ridge that filled the northern sky was a considerable formation, and rounding its southern end required a lot more travel than seemed likely at first glance, but the fugitives covered the distance in about fifteen minutes and arrived in an area where stretches of upland meadow went undulating back from the right-hand edge of the trail and soon rolled into the high plains on which the local cattlemen thrived.

Knowing the way to the Frayleson ranch house from the journeys of his childhood, Ames swung off the main trail onto a deep-worn path to his right and put his mount to the sandy, flint-studded middle of the track. He was conscious of sporadic outbursts of shooting from the rear, but no longer took any serious notice of the crackling explosions—since he was confident that he and his companion had gained rather than lost ground to the chase—and, his concentration ebbing a little as his curiosity grew, gazed up at what was now the western face of the ridge and the part of it in which the Fullwood gang's hideout was situated.

Narrowing his eyes, Ames tried to pinpoint the ledge which served the outlaws' cave, but soon realized why movement up there had never caught the attention of any observer down here, for the details of bluff and scree-slope, rift and storm-scoured rim, were so blurred by vapours and altitude that it was impossible to be sure where this or that particular began and ended. The heights were indeed just a featureless part of the Medicine Bow and might well keep a hundred secrets from the prying eyes of Mankind to the world's end.

The fugitives approached the top of their first climb, and Ames knew that he and Mary Frayleson were about to pass onto her father's ranchland. With any luck, it wouldn't be long now before they came upon members of the Circle F crew at work and were able to shout for assistance. Ames guessed that Joe Fullwood and company would be equally aware of this, and judged that, if they had any sense, they would abandon the chase about now and retreat to safer ground; so he cast another glance to his rear—seeing that the dark girl was in the act of doing the same—and was startled when a heavier and more solid gunshot than any which had gone before boomed out, a large calibre bullet whizzing audibly above crown and driving into the summit ahead.

Ames recognized the make of weapon that had fired the shot by its sound. It was a Springfield-Allin—Rex Mills' old army rifle without a doubt—and now he saw the man himself halted at the edge of the main trail below and aiming over the heads of Fullwood and company as they climbed their horses in pursuit of Mary Frayleson and himself. Feeling an inner chill, Ames knew that Mills was a formidable marksman with that single-shot weapon of such great range and accuracy, and he gritted his teeth and waited for the other to fire again.

Once more the Springfield-Allin boomed. Ames felt the jar of the bullet as it reduced a corner of his cantle to flying bits of wood and leather, diverting the missile just enough to miss his right hip. Close—that had been far too close; and kicking a little frantically, he forced his mount onto the summit ahead during the moments that the man below had to occupy himself with opening the breech of his rifle and making a reload.

Watching the dark girl from the corner of his left eye, Ames prayed that she too would manage to get a trifle extra out of her horse, for what they needed to do was surmount the ridge before Mills could take aim and trigger again. Beyond the summit, the land hollowed somewhat and then climbed towards the next eminence at a much shallower angle, which promised a certain amount of protection for the fleeing pair; but either Mary failed to push quite hard enough or her horse was too drained to respond to her goading, for she was still a good target against the brow of the land when Mills fired for the third time.

Ames heard the bullet strike flesh. The black mare folded instantly to the ground, and its mistress pitched over its right shoulder and came heavily to rest on her face in the grass adjacent. Reining back, Ames sprang out of his saddle and, upping the Winchester that he still held, blasted down the hill at Rex Mills, taking the hat off the man's head. He cocked the weapon anew, and was determined to make his next shot a killer, but this time the rifle clicked emptily and he was forced to cast it from him.

Kneeling now, he reached down the hillside, expecting the girl to raise her head and take his hand; but she remained inert and he perceived that she was bleeding badly from the mouth and nose.

This began to look like a done job.

NINE

The outlaws downhill of Ames were climbing their mounts swiftly upwards. Drawing his revolver, he broke open the weapon's loading gate and reloaded its fired chambers from his belt loops, truly thankful that the Colt which he had earlier picked up from beside Harry Simmonds' dead body was of the same calibre as the pistol that Rex Mills had taken from him. His thinking in the pressure of the moment was somewhat blurred, but he was determined that, if he must die, he was going to take one or two of his enemies with him. He did have the advantage of firing off raised ground, and that should prove a help for a little while—though perhaps a very little while—but it should require only a few seconds of accurate shooting to kill off a good slice of the opposition. Thus he held his crouch and set himself, preparing to give battle, while still keeping an eye on the clearly rattled Rex Mills, who had, remarkably enough, gone seeking his hat and now appeared content to let his outlaw friends do the fighting.

After a few moments more, the ascending riders, pleased to hold their fire while Mills had been blasting over their heads, opened up again in earnest, and Ames heard the zip and smack of bullets around him. Throat tight and chest about the same, Ames braved the flying slugs and held his fire, willing to risk the telling hit in order to get all he could out of the six shots available to him; and the horsemen were within twenty yards of him when he marked his first target—a young, broad-shouldered man of whom he had previously taken slight account—and fired at him off a steady hand. The shot, meant to kill, didn't fly quite true, but it hit the young man in the right arm and caused him to so mismanage his horse after the impact that he turned it across the paths of the two riders following him and brought all three of them down.

Obviously no hero when faced with close action, Joe Fullwood, out ahead of his men by only a yard or so, sensed the disaster at his rear and, swearing audibly, yanked his mount aside, turning it back on its course and then circling behind the kick up of equine legs and human scrambling which had resulted from the collision of a moment or two ago, firing as he moved, but his shooting was largely uncontrolled and his bullets all missed Ames by wide margins.

Ames sighted on the gang-boss, following Fullwood with the muzzle of his gun, and triggered when he thought he had the other precisely in line. His bullet raked across Fullwood's chest, branding the man's shirtfront and causing blood to well up, but the wound was clearly not bad enough to make any difference, and Ames was forced to look on in frustration as the gang-boss again swung away from him and entered the reverse of his recent curve, once more obtaining some cover from the men and horses on the ground. 'Get up, you clumsy varmints!' he roared. 'You won't do any good lying down there!'

The three fallen outlaws and their mounts were in fact already rising, and the men immediately began to shoot towards the hilltop again.

'Charge him!' Fullwood yelled. 'He's only one man, god-dammit!'

That was a fact—and Ames could think of no cause to celebrate it—but he had obviously shown enough skill with his gun to impress the men below, for they held back and used their milling horses as cover while firing snap shots at him. Baffled by this kind of hide-and-seek, Ames nevertheless perceived the need to keep his enemies dodging with return fire, while noting apprehensively that Rex Mills—with both hat and nerve apparently restored—was galloping up the hill over to the right and clearly meant to swing in from that side and cut him down while the outlaws were distracting him from the front. It all seemed to be happening at top speed now, and Ames was aware that he could not expect to last much longer.

Then he saw that Mary Frayleson was stirring in the grass below him. She lifted her head and gazed at him dazedly, but there was also a full awareness of their plight in her eyes. Ames put out his left hand, reaching down towards her again. 'Let me help you!' he urged.

Placing her fingers in his, she came erect, her legs shaky, and he drew her onto the summit beside him. She stood there gasping, her eyes questioning, and he jerked his chin to the left, indicating the spot to his rear where his horse had earlier come to a stop. 'There you go!' he pressed once more. 'Get on that mount! Make a gallop for home! Snap it up!'

The girl tried to run to the horse, but her legs were still weak and Ames could see that she wasn't going to make it. Running up behind her, he put his hands under her armpits and gave her all the support he could. This enabled her to keep stumbling forwards, and they came to the mount and Mary caught up the reins and lifted a foot towards the near side stirrup; but again the effort was too much for her; and Ames was beginning to fear that success was after all beyond them, when a sudden peremptory command form nearby brought all noise and motion to a stop, signifying the end of the battle for the outlaws. Now Mary Frayleson sank to her knees and sobbed with relief as her baffled supporter released her torso and turned round to see what was happening.

Ames saw no instant reason for the cessation, but did see that Rex Mills was still on the move. The man had just spurred over the crest on his right and was charging straight at him, Colt raised and ready to fire. Ames tilted his own pistol upwards and snapped one off, striving to get in first, and he did better than he expected, for the onrushing horse cartwheeled in midcharge and hurled its rider out of the saddle. Mills struck hard and came somersaulting across the earth to end up spreadeagled at Ames's feet. Ames backed up a trifle, the better to cover his man—if there was a need—then stirred the other with a toe, uncertain as to whether he or the horse that lay nearby had received the bullet. Mills remained inert. There was no trace of a bullet wound on him. He was clearly knocked out, and Ames felt the bitter satisfaction of knowing that the other was still alive and would be there to face trial and the gallows in due course.

Stepping over the senseless Mills, Ames walked to the edge of the summit from which he had recently withdrawn to help Mary Frayleson. Now he saw what had brought the shooting to a stop, for Joe Fullwood and his surviving gangsters had their hands up and stood ringed by a party of pistol-pointing riders who wore the soiled garb of ranch hands. A fiery-eyed little man, brown as the proverbial berry, lantern-jawed and bent-nosed, was dominating things from the saddle of a chestnut gelding so large that it made him look like little more than a tall-hatted monkey sitting on its back. The small man kept jiggling at the hammer of his Colt and considering Joe Fullwood with a gaze which had the most profound dislike in it that Ames had ever seen. In fact Ames felt something so terrible in the stare that he was about to call and ask the man what it meant, when Mary Frayleson arrived at his side and declared: 'Josh Horner, you are the most welcome sight ever!'

'I guess me and the boys just happened to be riding the right part of the range for once, Miss Mary,' the other responded, grinning a monkey grin as he looked up at her. 'Are you all right? Your pa said you'd gone a-visitin' across the way.'

'Not quite,' Mary Frayleson returned ironically. 'Josh, I've heard some worrying talk about dad. Have you heard anything?'

'There's been bad news all right,' Horner answered, shifting uncomfortably in his saddle. 'We've had two gallopers in from town so far this day. From Albert Rutherford both. Your pa got shot this morning, Miss Mary, and was thought like to snuff it. That's what the first news was. The second was a heap more cheerful. Doc now figures your pa isn't as badly hurt as he seemed to begin with. He'll get right again. It may take a while—but he'll get right.'

'Thank goodness for that,' Mary Frayleson said.

'What's the story?' Horner asked curiously.

'Oh, Josh!' the girl pleaded. 'It's too long to recount here. Sufficient that those men are crooks.'

'I know they're crooks,' Horner responded. 'That's Joe Fullwood. He was a pest in Kansas, worse in Colorado, and he's been the plague itself up here in Wyoming. Him and his skunks shot a pal of mine who rode shotgun for Wells Fargo. I ain't forgotten, and won't. Fullwood ought to have been hung twenty years ago. If the town wants somebody to dump him, I'll do it—and thank the Council for the privilege.'

'I can testify that Joe Fullwood and his gang are the scum of Creation,' Mary Frayleson acknowledged. 'We must hand them over to the law as quickly as possible. Send a rider to town.'

'There's no longer any law in Brayton,' Ames said —'of the badge-wearing kind anyhow. As I reckon you know, Miss Frayleson, Hank Ames, my father, was bushwhacked by that hellion who's lying unconscious behind us.'

'From what I heard said in the cave,' the girl said gravely. 'Rex Mills has murdered the deputy sheriff too. Frank Broom had followed Laury Bergen up to the ridge on one occasion. That's what put Mills and the gang on to him.'

'I uncovered Frank Broom's body in the woods this morning,' Ames confirmed. 'Don't you recall what Laury Bergen told that bunch back in the cave? The town has sent out a posse to look for me. I wouldn't be surprised if it comes calling up here. You might as well lock up Fullwood and his boys for now. I've no doubt there's somewhere secure on your ranch.'

'There's somewhere secure,' Horner promised grimly. 'Hank Ames's boy, ain't you?'

'That's right—Jim.'

'I can remember you coming up here as a kid.'

'That I did,' Ames returned. 'But I don't remember you, Mr Horner. I suppose kids don't notice that much.'

'So your old man's dead? Frank Broom too?'

'That's the size of it.'

'Plenty big enough too,' Horner observed. 'I'm sorry about your dad, boy—and Frank Broom. Never a better pair. Sounds like all the more reason for a hanging.' He spat. 'A lynching would suit me better. That's the way we did it when me and Miss Mary's pa were your age. And a right good way it was too.'

'As to that, my father hated rough justice.'

'It was rough okay,' Horner agreed, grinning savagely. 'Tootin' for your pa's job, boy?'

'No,' Ames replied. 'Folk always think things like that. I've got a job back in Cheyenne.'

'I just figured the town could do worse,' Horner said inconsequentially. 'You seem to handle yourself well enough.'

'I want to avenge my father's murder,' Ames said simply, glancing round at Mary Frayleson. 'Wrongs have been done elsewhere too. We've got the villains responsible. That's what matters. All this talk adds nothing.'

'Take your point,' Horner said with finality, looking up and around him. 'This day will soon be coming to an end. Well, Miss Mary, you're in charge. Say what you want, and I'll get it done.'

'We'll take these crooks home,' the girl said. 'They can walk. Somebody else can bring their horses along.'

'Where'll you want 'em put when we get to the ranch, Miss Mary?'

'In the root cellar under the barn,' Mary Frayleson replied. 'With the trap battened down and somebody standing guard over it, they won't have any chance of getting out of there.'

'That's how I'd have figured it myself,' Horner commented, turning his head away and starting to give orders among the cowboys for watching over the outlaws during their walk to the ranch and the collection and care of the badmen's horses.

'Are you coming with us?' Mary Frayleson asked of Ames.

'I don't see what else,' he confessed, tossing back a faintly embarrassed laugh. 'Where's the sense hunting trouble? It's trouble I'd be likely to miss anyway.'

'You don't sound in any hurry to meet up with that posse from town,' Mary observed curiously.

'They always were a misbelieving horde in Brayton,' Ames explained. 'Fred Parfitt, the mayor, is likely heading the posse. He always did want to know the answer to every question that was ever asked. "Why'd you run off, Jimmy?" " 'Cos I knew you'd clip my wings, sir." Then he'll ask why I should care about having my wings clipped, since the affairs of the law are no affair of mine. Answer—Oh, hell!'

'What is or was the answer, Mr Ames?'

'I'd found out about you from my father's log,' Ames replied. 'Please don't call me Mr Ames. Mr Ames is dead. I'm Jim. Always was at your kitchen door.'

'Dad had told the sheriff about my kidnap?' the girl mused. 'That wasn't wise. He'd been warned against doing that.'

'What else was he to do?' Ames

demanded. 'Pay up? Why, sure! I haven't a doubt he'd have done that gladly—and far more besides—if that had been all. But I've also no doubt that deep down he feared what I feared. Even if those crooks had been paid their ransom money, they'd have ended up slaying both you and him. You knew their identities, and the West is getting too small to hold their kind any more.'

'As it turned out, I suppose the poor man acted for the best.'

'How often are we sure?' Ames sighed. 'Yes, it turned out right—so why ponder what might have happened if it hadn't?'

A shout from Josh Horner echoed to them up the hillside. 'We're ready to move off, Miss Mary!'

The girl waved to him. 'All right!'

'We mustn't forget about Mills,' Ames reminded, turning to where the man he'd named still lay senseless.

'Can't you throw him on your horse, Jim?'

'That's what I'll do,' he agreed, stepping up to Mills' motionless shape, seizing the man under the armpits, dragging him to the overo, then picking him up and pitching him face down across the mount's saddle. That done, Ames went to the animal's head and began leading it after Mary Frayleson, who had already set off on foot across the high pastures and was showing the way to all concerned.

Before long, moving as a procession of sorts, the party reached and crossed the main land crest of the area and then advanced steadily down the shallow reverse slope. A magnificent view of the Medicine Bow peak itself was now present. The mountain's white cone floated above the green miles ahead and told why Jeff Frayleson had picked this spot to build his cattle business. There could be no place in the Northwest more fertile and beautiful than this. Ames reflected that only a man without a soul would fail to be gladdened as he gazed at the pastille freshness of the ice-ridged horizon out there and the flawless purple of the evening sky above it. The voice of the booming north seemed to be frozen into that mighty silence.

It had been a long and trying day, but it seemed to have been one of victory too. Ames knew that it might be days hence before he fully realized what he had achieved during this one. He had suffered a certain amount of physical damage, but felt no pain, and he strode along as the girl ahead of him strode along, content to enjoy the hour and the full use of his limbs. His imagination, still burning with a nervous fire, wanted to fight the battle from which he had just emerged over again. He wouldn't let it happen. For he realized how fortunate he had been to avoid death or a serious wound, and he wanted to go on carrying the illusion that he possessed a charmed life. He might well need it again in the future. Being a bank guard was not without its hazards. Reports were always coming in from somewhere in the country that one or more of the breed had died in a raid. You got a little superstitious about these matters when you spent your working days in an environment where Death was a likely caller. If what he was suffering from right now was anti-climax, he could stand a lot of anti-climax.

They moved off the downgrade. Now he saw a sheltered place ahead. In its banked hollow a cluster of corrals and ranch buildings stood. Ames nodded to himself. This was the Circle F home ground all right. It was much as he recalled, but seemed smaller and less imposing than of old. Yet he supposed that the change must be in his adult eye, for the house, barn, and crew quarters stood exactly as before. They were virtually untouched by the years and likely to stand for generations to come. He tried to look forward into the next century—attempting to imagine what 'progress' would do to this place and cattle raising generally—but he reckoned that any change here would spoil rather than improve. This green corner of Wyoming was about as perfect as he would want any place to be. Which was the more remarkable because he didn't often have such thoughts.

Soon they arrived on the ranch site. A black and white Welsh collie dog ran to meet them from the house. Barking its delight, it jumped up the front of Mary Frayleson's skirt. Laughing aloud, the girl made as much fuss of the animal as it made of her, and they slanted towards the house, the dog continuing to dance around Mary and make a joyous nuisance of itself, and she was content to push open the kitchen door and go inside without looking back.

This left Ames holding the horse that still had Rex Mills bent across its back and feeling rather uncomfortable. He had no clear idea of what he ought to do next. He seemed superfluous to everybody's need, so he held back a little now and wandered after Josh Horner and the cowboys present as they herded the prisoners into the eastern end of the Circle F's great barn and opened the root cellar there, a process which Ames was able to watch through the gap left between the leaves of the big door which served that end of the building.

Horner had the outlaws lined up opposite the open trap. Then he ordered one of the cowboys down into the cellar with instructions to light a lantern there and make sure that there were no implements around which the badmen could use offensively. The man reappeared about a minute later, reporting all serene, and Joe Fullwood and his three companions capable of descending the steps were driven into the depths. Horner watched them disappear, then turned and walked out of the barn to where Ames was standing with the overo and its limp burden. 'We could chuck that cuss down the old well,' he said harshly. 'Best place for him.' After that he stalked along the off side of the colourful horse and lifted Rex Mills' head, first looking into the man's pale face and then examining the skull beneath the other's pomaded hair with fingers that were far from gentle.

'Well?' Ames prompted, after a few moments.

'He's got a pretty fair bump over the forehead,' Horner commented. 'What exactly happened? I couldn't see properly up where you and Miss Mary were.'

Ames told how his bullet had fetched Mills' horse down, with the present consequences to its rider.

'Pity he didn't break his blasted neck!' Horner acknowledged unfeelingly. 'He could have a fractured skull, I suppose. I reckon he needs a doctor. We can't just pack him off with that scum down there. Ain't done. Oughta be—but ain't! Where to put the long son-of-a-bitch, that's the question.' He knocked back his Stetson and scratched his head, sniffing with embarrassment as he saw that Mary Frayleson and the black and white collie dog had joined them while he was speaking. 'No disrespects meant to you, Nettie,' he said to the animal. 'And apologies for the language, Miss Mary.'

'Well, he *is* a human being,' the girl

stressed, smiling wryly. 'I know that's not much credit to the rest of us, but there you are. He'd better be brought into the house. I'll send a man into Brayton for Doctor Rutherford.'

'Ain't you taking a bit of a risk there?' Horner asked rather bluntly. 'I wouldn't give the bas—I wouldn't give the guy kennelroom—again with no disrespect meant to the dog. Even if he was a week dead, I'd take no chances and nail him down!'

'You'd probably be right,' Mary Frayleson sighed. 'But you'd better bring him into the house all the same. Jim Ames will be there, keeping me company, so we shouldn't worry too much about what Mills could do. I don't think he looks capable of any more wickedness today anyhow.'

'If that's what you want, Miss Mary,' Horner said fatalistically. 'Okay, Ames. Fetch that fancy cayuse of yours along to the back door.'

Ames turned the overo away from the barn. Then he led it in the wake of Mary Frayleson and the man who was obviously her foreman. They walked down the yard at the rear of the ranch house and came

179

to the back door. Ames stopped the horse on the ground most convenient to the step and, glancing over his shoulder, watched the girl pass into the kitchen. There she faced about on the floor of red flagstones and said: 'We won't put him upstairs. I feel that could prove a little too tempting. The couch in the parlour is a nice big one. Dad often stretches out on it himself. We'll put Mills on that.'

Horner nodded. 'Let's have him off your saddle, Ames.'

'Very good,' Ames acknowledged; and he lifted the injured man off the overo; and then Horner and he carried Mills indoors between them.

They crossed the kitchen. Mary Frayleson opened a door at the back of the room and let them into the hall beyond. Here they moved towards the front of the house and passed into a large and comfortably furnished room on the left, where a large bay window provided a wonderful view of the pinnacle of the Medicine Bow and the rugged uplands adjoining. The couch mentioned by the girl stood before a hearth about which brasses were prominent. Ames and Horner placed the hurt man upon the thickly stuffed seat, then covered him with a blanket which Mary Frayleson supplied. The daughter of the ranch stood by and shook her head over the sight—for Mills was a handsome devil in his helplessness—and then she said: 'Send Ray Calder into town, Josh. He's our fastest rider, and Mills obviously needs medical help as soon as possible.'

'One of those men down in the root cellar has got a bullet in the arm,' Ames reminded, 'and I noticed that Joe Fullwood was still bleeding a lot.'

Mary Frayleson glanced at Ames's bloodstained shirt. 'You need attention too.'

'There's doctoring enough here,' Horner observed, 'for old Rutherford to work up quite a bill.' He began heading for the door, craning as he went. 'You might include yourself in, Miss Mary. You've got a fat lip and a cut nostril.'

'Less of your cheek, Josh Horner!' Mary said sternly, making a sign to the dog, which had never been far from her. 'See him off, Nettie! Then go and keep an eye on those villains we've got imprisoned in the barn!'

The dog made a playful dive for Horner's backside, then dodged the casual foot he swung at it and went out of the door ahead of him, clearly with a full understanding of the orders it had been given.

Ames yawned, feeling a sudden reaction to all his exercise of late.

'Sit down, Jim,' Mary Frayleson advised.

Nodding his thanks, he took a chair.

'I'll make some coffee,' the girl said.

But no sooner had the girl left the room than his chin rolled across his chest and he was asleep.

TEN

Ames came awake with a guilty start. He realized that it was no compliment to the lady of the house when a guy went off to sleep in her parlour. Then, as he opened his eyes—relieving his lungs in a huge yawn—he saw that there was now a fire blazing in the grate, the curtains were drawn at the window, and the lamps were burning in their various stations around the room. Blinking, he saw Mary Frayleson sitting in the chair opposite him, a pistol upon her lap and, as their eyes met, she smiled a little and said: 'My word! You have had a good sleep!'

'Sure have,' he agreed, stirring sluggishly and suspecting that he was owl-eyed. 'Reckon it's all this excitement.' He glanced at the couch, where Rex Mills still lay motionless. 'Has he come round at all?'

'He stirred about an hour ago, but slipped away again.'

'The doctor hasn't seen him yet?'

'He hasn't got here yet,' the girl explained. 'He was probably still out on his rounds when Ray Calder got to town. It happens. But fortunately we don't need a doctor too often.'

'What's the time?'

Mary Frayleson glanced at the cuckoo clock above the sideboard. 'Just after nine o'clock. There's been no sign of the town posse either.'

'There's no guarantee they'll come here,' Ames said, giving his arms a stretch. 'It was just a thought I had. I expect we shall have to take those outlaws to town ourselves in the end. I'll do it myself in the morning, if you'll kindly supply the transport.'

She nodded. 'I know you're wary of

going into Brayton.'

'Uneasy about it,' he corrected. 'I've got to go there finally, haven't I?'

'Your home's there,' she agreed. 'What will you do about that?'

'How d'you mean?'

'I got the impression you didn't want to leave your job in Cheyenne,' the girl responded. 'Will you close the house or sell up?'

'That's one I have to wrestle with,' Ames confessed. 'Yet I guess it's no contest. I'll have to sell up.' He frowned to himself. 'Gosh, that hurts! I didn't think I'd feel it quite so much.'

'Your father hasn't been dead long, has he?'

'It'll probably get worse before it gets better,' Ames agreed. 'I'll miss the old guy, that's for sure. Home is home and all that; but Cheyenne has everything.'

'Wine, women, and song?'

'All that too.'

'You men!'

'I've been real virtuous,' Ames protested jocularly. 'I was fixed to marry Laury Bergen, and I lived up to my part. I wonder where the dickens that girl is tonight?'

'Is it important to you, Jim?'

'Who wants to see a woman hanged?' he asked, feeling sick inside. 'I hope she rides the sun down. Pray God she's got that much sense. I hope to goodness I never see her again. I loathe where I loved. How can that be? It shouldn't.'

'There are rules,' Mary Frayleson said. 'There are rules to every mortal thing. You can't make anything good in this world without there first being rules. From a marriage to a steamboat.'

He chuckled at the apparent absurdity of her examples. 'I reckon I cotton to your drift. Laury sure tossed that rule book away. She was always the headstrong one. I expect she figured she'd always get away with it. I hope for her sake she's now learned better.'

'Do people like that ever learn?' Mary asked thoughtfully, stiffening in her chair as scratching noises and an anxious canine whining sounded at the back door. 'What's that? It sounds like Nettie! She must have got tired of the job I set her. I expect the poor thing wants some food.'

'Maybe,' Ames said uncertainly, since he knew little of the dog or the set up here.

Mary Frayleson rose to her feet. Leaving

the gun from her lap on the seat behind her, she walked quickly out of the room, heading for the kitchen. Prompted by a curious alertness that he could not quite explain, Ames strode after her and came to a stop in the doorway at the rear of the kitchen. He stood and watched the girl as she opened the back door.

Next moment the dog came bounding inside. It sprang up at Mary in a terrible state of urgency, front paws striking her chest and tongue licking her face, and all the time it seemed to be crying and yelping out a frantic message. 'There's something wrong over at the barn!' the girl called across her shoulder, features now tense and strained in the light of the single small lamp by which the kitchen was illuminated.

A shot boomed outside in the dark, and the bullet came indoors and struck the floor under the collie's body, bits of broken tile stinging the dog up and causing it to go yelping deeper into the house for safety. 'That consarned hound!' roared a deep male voice that was unmistakably Joe Fullwood's.

Crying out in fright, Mary Frayleson slammed the back door and contrived to spin the retaining bar into its iron slots an instant before the woodwork shuddered under the impact of a powerful shoulder. 'God-dammit-to-hell-and-gone!' Fullwood's voice now raved, his frustration obviously screwed to a brain-bursting pitch. 'Open that door, Hob curse you, girl!'

Ames sensed what was coming. He sprang across the room and seized Mary around the middle. Then he swung her clear of the woodwork and spun them into the shelter of the stone wall beside the door.

The gun outside spoke again, and its snarling crack emphasized the dreadful rage behind it. Shot after shot punched through the door, blasting the back of the woodwork into a state of yellow rents and flying splinters. The slugs hammered the objects and walls beyond, ricochets howling amidst the stench of burned powder which found its way indoors behind the roaring discharges.

Ames put the girl from him as the firing stopped in a succession of metallic clicks. Drawing his own revolver, he spun to his right and faced the door, sure that Fullwood was standing close behind the torn woodwork and right in the path of the shots that he intended to fan off. But then he sensed a movement behind him and heard Rex Mills' voice say thickly: 'Drop it, Jimmy, and get your hands up! You, Mary Frayleson—unbar the door!'

Craning, Ames let his revolver fall at his feet and raised his arms. He glimpsed Mills standing in the hall doorway and covering them with the pistol that Mary had left on the seat of her chair in the parlour.

'The wretch was foxing!' the girl complained bitterly, returning to the back door and restoring the retaining bar to its open position.

'Might have known it,' Ames agreed.

Now the back door burst open. Joe Fullwood came blundering into the kitchen. His features still wore the choler of one half beside himself. He shoved his empty Colt—doubtless obtained from a guard during his as yet unexplained escape from the root cellar—into his belt, then let fly at Mary with a terrific backhander. The girl reeled away from the blow, crying out, and almost fell, but she fended herself off the floor with her right hand and straightened up again, looking Fullwood proudly in the eye as she said: 'Coward!'

'I'll give you coward!' the gang-boss

grated, making to strike her again; but then Laury Bergen—looking quite old and burned out in that moment—appeared, suddenly on the back doorstep and cried: 'Joe, you haven't got time for that! Seize her and ride away! Use the horse standing out here!'

Fullwood lost colour and his chest swelled visibly as he regained control of himself. 'You're right, Laury,' he admitted, then gave a shout of pain as Mary's dog, Nettie, came diving out of the hall—passing Mills like a flash—and sank its teeth into the gang-boss's swiftly thrown up left arm.

A very strong man whatever else, Fullwood jerked up to his full height and braced himself, throwing the dog off him and then kicking it savagely in the belly. The collie rolled over and over on the floor, yelping, but was up again in a moment or so and dodging very neatly as Fullwood closed in to stamp the life out of it. Avoiding the badman, the animal jumped through his legs and, swerving round Laury Bergen on the doorstep, vanished into the darkness of the ranch yard.

Off balance from his poorly controlled attack on the collie, Fullwood staggered between Ames and Mills for a moment. Ames took his chance and, dipping at the knees, snatched up his revolver from the floor, side-stepping the gang-boss's reeling figure and firing at the startled Mills as the man became a clear target.

Mills tried to avoid the shot, but the idea was in his mind and not his legs. He shuddered as the slug hit him squarely, and looked down as blood began spurting out of a hole close to his heart. Now he made a great effort to bring the muzzle of his pistol round, but it was too late, for his knees were already buckling, and the shot that he had fought so hard to trigger off drove into the floor just an instant before he measured his length there and twitched into stillness.

Facing left, Ames switched his full attention to Joe Fullwood, but it had been the gang-boss's turn to use a vital second to the maximum advantage. For he had already grabbed Mary Frayleson round the body and was retreating through the back door with her person as a shield. Ames lifted his gun. He was certain that he could put a bullet through Fullwood's head at this range with little risk to Mary, but the boss outlaw instantly saw his purpose and seized the girl's chin with his right hand, wrenching hard enough to make his counter intention plain. 'Try that, boy,' he warned, 'and I'll break her neck!'

Ames held his fire. He dared not risk it. The gang-boss, eyes steely, had just pulled his head down behind the girl's and made a minimum target of it. Now the pair were off the step and into the yard, and Laury Bergen stepped up from the moon-touched gloom on the right of the exit and yanked the back door shut. This cut Ames off from any glimpse of what was happening outside.

Feeling a moment of deep uncertainty, he stood rooted. All he had to do was open the door again, but he would be standing against the light in here and an easy target for anybody waiting out there with a gun. Then he heard the dog snarling again, and the cry of pain which came from Laury Bergen was a loud and agonized one. The collie had evidently decided that the girl would make the easiest mark for its renewed attack, and Ames felt reasonably certain that this activity would be drawing more attention outside than the reopening of the kitchen door would be likely to occasion. So he opened the door, sinking low as light shafted out into the night, conscious at once of a nearby Laury under assault from the dog's jaws and beating at the animal with a hand as she tried to climb astride her horse, which was standing only a yard or two short of the overo that Fullwood was just now attempting to appropriate for Mary Frayleson and himself.

Eluding the collie for a moment, Laury Bergen did her best to spring onto her horse in a masculine way, but her clothing was not cut for that type of exercise and, as she lost her balance beside a mount which was already on the move, the dog skipped in again and nipped the horse's hindquarters. Whinnying its fright, the mount lunged forward, and Laury lost her grip on it completely. She fell flat on her face, and the animal surged away from her and passed around the northern end of the house, where Josh Horner could now be heard shouting orders and firing had just broken out.

Ames glimpsed Laury rising. She was little better than a black shadow in fact, and sobbing with fear. He sprang forward and made a grab at her, but she evaded his grasp with a rapid duck and twist; then, fully erect now and running flat out, she began fading into the big splash of night at the top end of the yard which the slice of moon riding low to his right was hardly lighting at all.

He felt the temptation to chase Laury, but decided to let her go for the moment. The dog had just turned its attention to the horse—Ames's own mount—which Joe Fullwood, firm in the saddle now, had been fighting to spur clear of the yard for about half a minute. He had so far been checked in this by the convulsive exertions of the female captive whom he had seated in front of him. The gang-boss kept cursing Mary Frayleson and doing his best to clamp down her struggling limbs, and he could have been nearing success, when the collie sank its teeth into one of the mount's back legs and hung on for all it was worth.

The effect of the canine attack was practically eruptive. Up went the overo, squealing its pain and fury as it towered to within a degree of the vertical, and out of its saddle shot both Fullwood and the girl. The gang-boss landed hard enough on his own account, but the force of the impact was almost doubled when Mary Frayleson came to rest upon his face in a sitting position. Even so, strong indeed—as demonstrated before—he stirred within moments and, pitching the girl off him, staggered to his feet and gathered himself to attempt running away from the scene.

Ames went for the man. Fullwood swung at him. Blocking the punch, Ames struck at the outlaw with the barrel of the gun that he was still holding in his right hand. The muzzle of the weapon skidded across the top of Fullwood's skull, stunning the man to the point of senselessness—but he wouldn't go down; and, fearing that he might brain the other if he repeated the dose more precisely, Ames stepped in and hooked with his left, flooring the gang-boss with the kind of punch from which no man was going to get up. Fullwood lay stretched upon his back, and Ames was confident that the outlaw was going to remain unconscious for a long time to come.

Going up to Mary Frayleson now, Ames helped the young woman to her feet. 'All right?' he inquired anxiously.

'I—I think so,' she faltered. 'Yes, I'll—I'll be all right. Is that—Is that it, Jim?'

Ames lifted his voice. 'Horner!'

'Hello!' came the response. 'That you hollering, Ames?'

'I haven't heard a peep out of anybody else!' Ames responded dryly. 'I imagine you've fixed the rest?'

'Depends on what you've fixed!'

'Mills and Fullwood!'

'Yeah, we've fixed the rest!'

It was Mary Frayleson's turn to raise her voice. 'Come here, Josh!'

Footfalls dutifully approached, running. 'Yes, Miss Mary?'

'What happened over at the barn, Josh?'

Horner had halted a few feet away, and he was slow to reply.

'It must have been Laury Bergen,' Ames responded.

'Well, that's it,' Horner agreed. 'I'm not altogether sure what did happen yet. But—it must have been the girl. Those of us in the bunkhouse heard Nettie barking. I knew she was sitting with the man on guard in the barn, and it figured there was a rescue attempt on. Me and the men ran over there, and sure enough that's what we found. The guard was lying beside the trapdoor, out for the count, and those bad guys were up from the cellar and spitting, but they sure as hell didn't know what they were about. They ran this way and they ran that, but we rounded them up right away. Aw, it's all a bit muddled around the edges, but we'll get it sorted in due course.'

'You fellows did very well, Horner,' Ames praised. 'All we have to do now is catch Miss Bergen by the ankle. I wonder where the heck she ran to?'

'That's simple,' Horner said, jerking a thumb over his shoulder. 'I saw her run into the barn.'

'I had her down for smarter than that.'

'Everything about her looked scared,' Horner said. 'Going in there, boy?'

'Yes.'

'I'll come too.'

'Might be better if you left it to me.'

'Sure, she's just a girl,' Horner said. 'Is she armed?'

'I'm pretty sure not.'

'You men!' Mary Frayleson sighed bitterly. 'You will underestimate the members of my sex!'

'I underestimate nobody,' Ames said, holstering his gun, as if to contradict his words. 'I'll see you both shortly. Keep an eye on Fullwood, eh?'

'Of course,' Mary said.

Ames walked quickly towards the barn. There were men moving in the vicinity but he ignored them. He entered the barn through the gap between the big leaves of the main door. There was ample light near the entrance by which to see, for a storm-lantern had been suspended from a nail knocked into one of the building's central uprights. Halting, Ames took down the lantern and adjusted its wick to give the best possible light. Then, with the source of illumination raised before him, he stepped into the gloom beyond at a slow but even rate. 'Laury!' he shouted. 'I know you're in here!'

He received no answer.

'Don't be difficult,' he warned. 'I'll find you. I'll look into every hole and corner—until I find you. So why not pack it in right now?'

Still there was no reply.

'Do we have to have more trouble?' Ames insisted. 'The case against you is clear. And you've damned well added to it by trying to free Fullwood and his boys. You're caught in all that matters, you know, and you'll have to answer. I can't say what your fate will be. You could dodge the hangman and get off with a few years in jail. Who knows? You're young and mighty good looking. Got to be worth a try!'

He heard a faint stirring ahead of him and high up. Pushing the rays from his lantern to their fullest extent, he saw that he was approaching the back of the hay loft's quarter floor and the fixed ladder leading up to it. Something whizzed momentarily, dropping sharply, and he halted abruptly as a pitchfork drove into the earth as his feet. 'That was close,' he said resignedly. 'But if that's how you want it!'

'It's not how I want it!' the girl suddenly responded chokily from the darkness of the loft. 'Let me go, Jim! I promise nobody about here will ever hear anything of me again.'

'You had your chance,' he reminded implacably. 'Why didn't you keep going after you got free?'

'We have to be loyal to our friends!'

'You couldn't manage without them!' Ames returned scathingly. 'You're an empty shell, and you've nothing of your own!'

'Please, Jim—please!'

He resumed advancing, making for the

foot of the ladder which served the hay loft.

'Jim, I'm afraid!'

'You're afraid to live, and afraid to die.'

'Jim!'

'It's out of my hands, Laury,' he said with finality, carefully holding his lantern level as he put a foot on the ladder and started to climb.

'Don't come up here!'

'I'm coming,' he said, ascending remorselessly.

'I'll—I'll kill you!'

'I doubt it,' he replied indifferently.

Then he was at the top of the ladder. It was here that he feared Laury might attack him. He still needed both hands to steady himself on the ladder, and a boot in the face would be difficult to avoid as he raised his head above the edge of the floor. It might not prove too difficult to dislodge him entirely, and the fall beneath would most probably kill him. But it didn't happen thus. There was no threatening movement towards the top of the ladder, and he was able to complete his ascent and step into the hay loft without interruption.

He raised the lantern high. It showed him a clear path across the floor ahead to the upper door at the back of the building through which hay was pitched and sacks of grain lifted and lowered by the chain hoist during the working day. He gazed around him, his light penetrative enough, and saw shapeless piles of hay and other formless objects on either hand, but no sign of the girl. Reckoning that she would reveal herself soon enough, Ames began walking towards the door opposite, listening for the tiniest sound which would tell him that Laury was on the move, but everything remained still and was all at once utterly tense.

Coming to the further end of the loft, Ames looked out briefly through the opening there, conscious of the moonlight dimly reflected off mountain clouds and of shadows settling blackly through the space beneath him, with the ground just visible as a solid blot where the drop ended. Now he experienced an instant of inner warning, for he had kept totally aware, and he heard light feet racing up from his rear. He spun away to his left, an extended hand brushing his right arm, and the recklessly charging Laury missed him with her shove and went plunging out into the night, her scream abruptly choked off amidst a rattling of chains, and Ames—horrified for all that he had anticipated tragedy—gazed out and down to see that the falling girl's head had become entangled with the hoist chains and that she was now swinging in mid-air, well and truly hanged. Poetic justice? It could be. And who was he to find fault with that?

He turned his head away from the sight and, breathing deeply, calmed himself. After that he walked back across the hay loft, descended the ladder to the ground floor of the barn and stepped outside, wondering whether he would ever know true peace of mind again. If ever love's dream had ended as a nightmare, his had. How could he have been so wrong in his judgment of a woman? When all was said and done, Laury Bergen's wickedness had been matched by his stupidity. The weaknesses in the girl's character had always been there; but, perceiving them, he had been blindly determined not to accept what they meant. Well, he could only put it down to experience. He was simply too young to let one miscalculation of the heart blight his whole life. He would get back to

Cheyenne as quickly as possible—put all this behind him. Things would probably fall back into place soon enough. They usually did.

Mary Frayleson and the dog, Nettie, met him at the back door of the ranch house. Ames told Mary what had happened in the barn, and she listened aghast. 'It's too awful!' she finally breathed.

'Mayhap for the best,' Ames said stonily. 'It's happened, anyhow, and we can't unhappen it.'

'No,' the girl agreed. 'There's some better news for you. Doctor Rutherford has arrived. He says my father has put on record exactly what passed between you and him in the sheriff's office. Concerning me. How he was shot in the back, too, by somebody he didn't see. You've nothing to worry about in Brayton. I don't think you ever had.'

'Fine,' Ames said—'just fine.'

'I've made some fresh coffee, Jim. Would you like a cup?'

He gave a relieved grin. You bet he would!

The publishers hope that this book has given you enjoyable reading. Large Print Books are especially designed to be as easy to see and hold as possible. If you wish a complete list of our books, please ask at your local library or write directly to: Dales Print Books, Long Preston, North Yorkshire, BD23 4ND, England.

This Large Print Book for the Partially sighted, who cannot read normal print, is published under the auspices of

THE ULVERSCROFT FOUNDATION